DEATH ORCHID

HAWAII THRILLER SERIES

J.E. TRENT

BONUS

Get the free prequel and new release notifications.
https://readerlinks.com/l/965413

1

LOS ANGELES

Detective Jessica Kealoha was meeting Special Agent Gabbie Harris for brunch at an outdoor café in Marina Del Rey next to the harbor. Jessica felt serene whenever she was near the ocean. She and Gabbie tried to meet there at least twice a month to have mimosas and blow off steam from the task force they had been assigned to work together on.

As Jessica made her way to the table on the outdoor patio where Gabbie sat, an ocean breeze blew through her hair. She loved the smell of the salt air because it reminded her of growing up in Hawaii.

It was an overcast sky in early June and the temperature was about eighty degrees that Sunday morning in southern California.

The June gloom from the marine layer was in full effect, and Jessica hated it with a passion because she suffered from depression on most of those gray days. Every June all she wanted to do was sleep through the overcast days until July and the return of blue skies.

The café was busy. The owner, Steve, was late-forties and always had a large table reserved on Sundays for an assortment of young women he was trying to sleep with. It was always full of the "beautiful people," as Gabbie liked to refer to them, mostly wannabe actresses with boob jobs and mini skirts that looked like someone had spray painted them on.

By contrast, Jessica wore jeans and a white t-shirt with tennis shoes. She had a subcompact 9mm in a belly band holster hidden under her t-shirt. Gabbie was going to work out afterward; she wore gym shorts and a tank top. Her 9mm was in her fanny pack.

Jessica had noticed Steve liked to chase women in their twenties and never hit on her or Gabbie since they were in their thirties. And they carried guns for a living.

A big crowd was there that day, and Jessica had to squeeze between two packed tables to get to where Gabbie sat. She was glad the diet of the week was finally starting to pay off, since there was a time when her hips might not have glided so easily between the close-together tables.

Jessica and Gabbie had been working together for a year now and had become close friends because they had similar interests outside of work. They talked about everything, not just work.

Gabbie was always trying to fix Jessica up with one of her husband's political colleagues, but Jessica only liked to date other cops.

Gabbie was taking a healthy gulp of her drink when Jessica sat down. Her eyes were puffy. It was obvious she had been crying.

Jessica's eyebrows furrowed when she saw Gabbie's face. "What happened?"

"Karl thinks I'm cheating on him with my trainer at the gym."

Jessica reached over and touched the side of Gabbie's face where it was obvious she had covered a bruise with makeup.

Gabbie looked down towards her drink sitting on the table, and tears began to run down her cheeks.

Jessica reached for Gabbie's hand. "Look at me. I know

you guys have been together since high school. But you have to leave him."

"I can't. I'm pregnant."

Jessica's eyes looked straight at the glass in front of Gabbie.

"It's only orange juice."

Jessica nodded.

&

TWO WEEKS later

Once again Gabbie had lied to the doctor about how she had broken her ribs. Karl made sure not to leave a mark on her face again. He was an expert at how to beat her up and not leave any signs of abuse. An abused wife with a black eye would be career ending for a Senator who campaigned on family values. Unseen injuries didn't require explanation.

But this time Senator Karl Harris had beaten Gabbie one too many times. Over and over through the years he'd sworn he'd never touch her again. This time she would hold him to it for sure. She instinctively knew the only way he would not beat her again was if he were dead. The trick would be to make it look like an accident.

Gabbie knew driving home from the hospital was the perfect time to ask Karl for something he would normally decline. His pattern after beating her had been to take her on a trip afterwards to make up and wash away his guilt. But this time it would be Gabbie who suggested the trip.

As she shifted in the car's seat trying to find a comfortable position, her broken ribs caused a sharp pain every time the car hit a bump in the road. She mustered as much sincerity as she could and said, "Honey, obviously you've been under a lot of pressure lately. Why don't we go to the Grand Canyon for a short vacation? We can take the train from Williams and spend two nights at the lodge at the South Rim of the canyon," Gabbie suggested.

"I don't know, Gabbie. I have a lot of work to do gearing up for my re-election campaign."

Karl paused for a minute and then said with a tone of voice as if he was doing her a favor:

"I suppose I could bring my laptop and do some work from the lodge." Gabbie nodded and turned her head to look at Karl. She smiled, thinking to herself that she'd had enough.

A Week Later

Jessica and Gabbie had cleared a big case that put a lot of Russian mobsters in prison and they were celebrating over dinner and drinks at a local brew pub.

"Karl and I are going by train to the Grand Canyon for a few days. He said he's going to be working on his computer most of the time and I don't want to be there by myself. Why don't you come along and we could see the sights together?" Gabbie said, while she was stirring her soup.

Jessica played with her salad before answering.

"I don't know, I don't want to be a third wheel."

"No, it will be fine, he'll just work all the time and I'll be alone if you don't come."

Jessica nodded. "Okay, if you're sure he won't have a fit, I'll tag along. I've always wanted to ride a train."

"You've never been on a train?"

"What can I say, I grew up on an island."

❧

KARL AND JESSICA traded dirty looks, while waiting at LAX to board their plane for the short flight to Phoenix. Jessica could tell Karl wasn't happy she came along, but she didn't care what he thought since Gabbie was her friend and needed her.

Jessica had never been to the Grand Canyon before, and

she was excited to get out and see the sights. She hardly slept the night before, and was awake at 5 a.m.; ready to go but it was still too dark outside. As soon as the morning light began to creep through the windows into her room, she was out the door and walking toward the rim of the canyon. She wanted to be alone the first time she saw the canyon, so she could enjoy the experience without interruption. Then later she would join Gabbie for whatever she wanted to do while Karl stayed in the lodge and worked on his campaign.

There was a small forest between the lodge and the rim of the canyon; the trees were thick and didn't let much light through. It was still so dark Jessica almost walked straight into a large elk grazing on the path a hundred yards from the lodge. She stopped in her tracks and waited for the enormous beast to move off of the trail so she could pass. She decided she didn't want to be at the whim of an unpredictable seven-hundred-pound animal, and doubled back to the lodge so she could take the long way around to the canyon.

Gabbie and Karl were coming out of their room and saw Jessica heading back in their direction.

"There's a big elk on the path. You might want to take the long way with me," Jessica said.

"We'll just have another cup of coffee and wait for it to pass." Karl said with a hint of annoyance.

"Okay, I'm off to find better coffee than what's in my room. We can meet up later."

Gabbie nodded and followed Karl back into their room.

Jessica headed off the long way to the coffee shop near the rim of the canyon.

An hour later she was walking along the rim heading back toward her room at the lodge, when she saw Karl and Gabbie about a hundred yards away. They were strolling toward a rock ledge that jutted out over the edge of the canyon. Jessica thought she would join them and started walking in their direction.

She was about fifty yards away when she saw Gabbie quickly step towards Karl just before he went over the edge. There was a large rock obstructing her view as she got closer to them. What wasn't clear to her was whether Karl had lost his balance and fell, or had been pushed. Gabbie had sat down at the edge of the ledge and watched the sun continue to rise and paint the walls of the canyon in orange and yellow hues. The canyon floor was a thousand feet below and showed Karl no mercy on that early autumn day.

When Jessica walked up, Gabbie sat there with tears streaming down her cheeks. Jessica sat down next to her and as she put her arm around Gabbie, her friend winced. Gabbie opened her jacket and lifted her shirt so Jessica could see the large bruises on her ribcage.

Jessica stared at the yellow and purple bruises and quietly asked, "How many times did he do this to you?"

"One too many. I lost the baby."

They sat there and continued to watch the sun rise and feel the warmth it provided from the early morning chill.

❦

JESSICA CALLED 911 and the park rangers arrived at the scene within a few minutes.

"It was a horrible accident," Gabbie told the ranger who was taking her statement as she sobbed. He took notes as he listened to Gabbie describe the accident. "Karl took a step, slipped and lost his balance, then fell over the edge," she continued.

A separate ranger interviewed Jessica.

"I was fifty yards away and didn't see it happen. I got a text and looked down to see who it was from, when I heard Gabbie scream; I looked up and Karl was gone."

The park rangers called for a helicopter to retrieve Karl's

body and told Gabbie, as gracefully as possible, it was going to cost her thirty-five hundred dollars to do so.

People slipped and fell in the canyon all the time. It happened so much there was even a book about all the deaths in the park that had happened that way.

It was an open and shut case as far as the rangers were concerned, and that was the end of it.

At Karl's funeral many fellow politicians testified to what a great loss his death was to the country. Jessica sat next to Gabbie and held her arm, careful not to brush against her broken ribs. They never spoke about it again but Jessica couldn't shake the thought Gabbie had pushed Karl to his death.

2

ISLAND OF HAWAII

One of the most remote and dangerous places on planet earth is the island of Hawaii. On the west side of the island is a small seaside fishing village called Kailua-Kona. To the locals it's known as "Kona."

The island is also known as the "Big Island" since it's big enough to hold all the other islands of Hawaii combined.

It is the island of fire and ice; from the flowing volcano to the snows of Mauna Kea. The terrain can go from a tropical paradise to hell on earth when the goddess of fire, Madame Pele, spews lava hundreds of feet into the sky.

Mother Nature has been known to show her best and worst, sometimes all on the same day.

She offers black sand beaches, turquoise blue water with palm trees and exotic tropical flowers.

Everything may look perfect, but there is always an underlying danger from the mountain to the sea.

Waterspouts, sharks, lava, earthquakes, and tsunamis. It can be a dangerous island.

3

SIX YEARS LATER – KONA, HAWAII

"Okay honey, I'll see you later," Jessica said just before she kissed Sam goodbye. He was going down to the boatyard to take care of a few technical details related to a new yacht design his company had been developing. The company had been working on it for months, and he wanted to get the bugs worked out before starting production.

While he was at work, Jessica spent the next hour and a half on the ocean in her canoe. Their house was at the water's edge of Keauhou Bay and she started her day by paddling five miles every morning. Some mornings a pod of dolphins escorted her as she paddled up to Lyman's Bay, where she liked to watch the surfers rip up and down the waves.

There was a cool, light breeze that morning coming off of the mountain toward the ocean. Instead of going north as usual, Jessica paddled south out of Keauhou Bay for a change of scenery. She skirted the shoreline as she paddled, being careful not to get too close to shore. The last thing she wanted to happen was being swept onto the jagged lava rocks that lined the coast in that area.

At the turnaround spot Jessica had stopped paddling to take a break before heading back. After a few minutes she was almost in a trance while admiring the beauty of the island from her drifting canoe. She snapped out of it when a flying fish sailed past her. It was only a few feet from the starboard side of the boat. The fish was trying to outrun a mahi-mahi that was doing its best to chase the smaller fish down for breakfast. It reminded her of chasing bad guys, in a weird sort of way. Not that the fish were good or bad, just the chase part triggered thoughts of her life before moving back to the island.

After the flying fish had skipped out of sight, she momentarily thought about how much her life had changed in the past year since retiring. It was so different from when she was an LAPD detective working in the Hollywood Robbery Homicide Division.

One of her biggest regrets was not spending more time with her father before his death. But she always thought of him when she paddled alone; it was an activity she and her sisters did with their father when they were growing up on the island. He had raised the girls around the sea their whole lives. From paddling to scuba diving, he had taught them well.

🐚

LATER THAT AFTERNOON Jessica was driving on the Queen 'K' highway on her way to meet Sam and the rest of the family at Aloha Village. Every time she drove past the lava flow, at the north end of the Kona Airport, she felt a heaviness. It was there where her father, Mike Murphy had died. He crashed his plane there, right after takeoff, because a jealous girlfriend had sabotaged it by putting sugar in the fuel tank.

Aloha Village was a few miles north of the airport on the ocean side of the highway. The small beachfront resort was an oasis surrounded by an old lava flow. It was a juxtaposition of the hot, arid surroundings and its sandy beach and coconut trees throughout the property.

The sky was postcard blue, punctuated with puffy clouds. It was in contrast to the somber mood she was in.

Jack Johnson's music always elevated her spirit. That day she turned on the stereo in her Jeep and selected "Banana Pancakes" from her Jack Johnson playlist. His music almost always helped her get her mind back in the right place.

Sam and Jessica arranged for a floating lantern ceremony to take place at four o'clock on the beach. It was to commemorate the one-year anniversary of the death of her father. After coming back from Vietnam, Mike Murphy married Jessica's mother in Japan, and became a Buddhist.

The vibe in the air was light. The family had gotten over the shock of Mike being taken from them.

The guests stood in little clumps, talking softly, while they waited for the ceremony to begin.

Jessica and Sam were talking about attending a fishing tournament in Mexico. Sam had fished the tournament the year before with Captain Steve Kaiser and had caught a nine hundred pound black marlin. He was telling her about the one that got away.

Jessica's sister Pua was chatting with a longtime return visitor of Aloha Village. She was trying to interest him in a condo she had just put on the market.

The youngest sister, Jasmine, was back on the island for the lantern float. She had been away attending veterinary school on the mainland. Pua's son, Kainoa, was helping Jasmine get the lanterns ready to launch.

Close to three hundred people jammed the small crescent-shaped beach fronting the resort.

People from all over the world attended. Most of them had missed the funeral the year before. Many were longtime guests of Aloha Village. They came to pay their respects to a man highly thought of when it came to preserving the island for generations to come.

❦

THAT EVENING SAM and Jessica were going to an important business meeting with Larry Black. Sam left right after the ceremony to again stop by the boatyard, but this time to review plans for a new super yacht design he was presenting to Larry that evening.

On the way home Jessica's phone rang. She tapped the screen of the Jeep's multimedia center to answer when she saw it was Aimee.

"What's up, Aimee?"

"I need a ride to an AA meeting tonight. I just tried to go deliver an order of purple orchids and my car won't start."

"I'm on the way home now. I'll pick you up, and we can drop off the orchids, then hang out for a while. Sam and I will give you a ride to the meeting when we leave for our business dinner."

"Nice, mahalos! I told my customer it would be over my dead body their order wouldn't get delivered today."

Fifteen minutes after picking up Aimee, Jessica turned off the highway and headed down the hill toward lower Keauhou. As she and Aimee talked about Aimee getting her son back, if she could stay sober, her Jeep's speed crept up toward 60 mph.

Noticing her speed, she stepped on the brake pedal to slow down before the curve in the road ahead. Nothing happened, except a sharp pang in her gut caused by the fear of not being able to stop.

She pressed the electronic parking brake switch with the same result, nothing. It was almost like throwing a bucket of water on a forest fire; too little, too late. They were heading down one of the steepest roads in Kona, Kam lll as the locals referred to it. It was short for Kamehameha lll. She and Aimee were most likely going to die if she couldn't get the Jeep stopped before the bottom of the hill.

❧

IVAN VOLKOV'S plan was for Jessica Kealoha to die a violent death while he watched it on his laptop computer in the air-conditioned comfort of his hotel room.

He had stalked Jessica for a week after he landed on the island. The first thing he did was to attach a custom-built GPS tracking device to her Jeep after he had followed her to the grocery store.

After mapping her routine for a week he waited until she went to the gym to plant a hidden camera in the grill of her Jeep. It was the perfect place to put it so he could watch the final moments of her life.

She had to pay for his brother's death. Unlike his brother, Vlad, Ivan wasn't a hitman by trade. He was a computer hacker who worked for the Russian government as a contract employee, and he was seeking revenge for his brother's death.

His mission was to hack the onboard computer of Jessica's Jeep and take control of it while she was driving. The final part of the plan was to kill her and make it look like an accident.

❧

THE JEEP BARRELED down the hill and gained more speed. Jessica had seconds to decide whether she and Aimee should jump. Or drive off the side of the hill into the jagged rocks of the lava flow.

The Jeep continued to speed up as it headed down the

steep hill toward the bend in the road, when she saw the
school bus.

It was waiting to turn left in the middle of the intersection.
The bus was three or four hundred yards away; she made the
only choice she could.

Jessica checked the tension on her seat belt and told Aimee
to do the same and yelled "Hold on!" She cranked hard on
the steering wheel to the right and hoped it would not be the
last thing she ever did.

Both of the side and front airbags deployed when the Jeep
smashed through the guardrail and into the first big rock.
Many more boulders were to follow as the Jeep rolled over
and over down the jagged slope of the old lava flow. Jessica
lost consciousness after the vehicle rolled for the third time,
and came to rest against a tree that kept it from continuing
any farther down the embankment.

A couple minutes later, after she had regained consciousness, she cracked one eyelid open and wiped the blood away
so she could see. The hardtop roof of the Jeep was pushing
her head down toward the steering wheel. The wreckage had
pinned her left hand and legs to where she couldn't move
them. And her cell phone was nowhere in sight. About right
then she wished she had bought the Chevy Tahoe with
OnStar instead.

She wiggled her toes and fingers to take an inventory of
her body parts. The good news was she wasn't missing
anything, and she still had some feeling in all of her limbs.

The crash shattered all the windows of the Jeep. Her forehead was cut by flying glass and her face covered in blood.
She was lucky a good Samaritan saw the crash and called 911.
Otherwise she and Aimee could have been down in the
ravine out of sight for hours before being discovered; if not
for days.

"Aimee, Aimee, are you okay?"

There was no answer.

Jessica felt Aimee's wrist for a pulse and couldn't find one. Aimee was dead–she still had a purple orchid clenched in her hand. An autopsy later would reveal she died of a broken neck from the crushed roof.

The doors wouldn't open; they were bashed in from the boulders as the Jeep rolled over them multiple times.

While trapped by the steering column, as she waited for help to arrive, Jessica had time to think about what caused the crash.

She wondered if someone had sabotaged the brakes on her SUV; brakes don't just 'go out' on a vehicle with less than ten thousand miles on it. And if so, by whom?

As the fire department worked to cut Jessica and Aimee from the wreckage, she knew it was a miracle she had no broken bones but her heart sank as she looked at the lifeless body of her friend.

4

Sam was on his way home from the boatyard when he passed by the scene of the accident. A policeman was directing traffic. Cars slowly inched by where the officer was standing. It never occurred to him that Jessica could be involved.

Since he couldn't see the mangled Jeep from the road, he was unaware that the fire department rescue squad was working to free her with the Jaws of Life. He passed by without a clue of what was happening to the love of his life.

When he got home and pulled into the driveway, he wondered where Jessica's Jeep was; she should have been home by now from Aloha Village.

After he walked into the house, he saw that the housekeeper was still there; he motioned to her to stop vacuuming for a minute.

"Has Jessica been home?"

The woman shook her head no and went back to vacuuming the living room rug.

Sam's phone buzzed, and by the time he pulled it out of his pocket it was too late to answer, but there was a voice message. He didn't recognize the number, but the message was chilling.

Jessica Kealoha has been in an accident and is on the way to the Kona hospital.

The thought of Jessica being injured made Sam's gut ache with fear. He raced on the way to the hospital until he hit the Kainaliu crawl. It was in full effect with cars moving at a snail's pace through the narrow, two-lane road that wound through coffee land.

Twenty-five minutes later, after arriving at the hospital, Sam rushed inside to the information desk.

"I'm looking for my wife, her name is Jessica Kealoha."

He lied to the receptionist because he knew she wouldn't give him any information if he wasn't her husband or immediate family. He decided if Jessica didn't die, he would make it official sooner than later. They weren't engaged, but he would remedy that after she recovered, he swore to himself. He couldn't stand the thought of losing her.

The receptionist picked up the phone and made a quick call. After confirming with someone on the other end of the line she said, "She's in the ER. There's a problem with the CT machine and they're trying to figure out what to do about it."

"Which way is the ER?" Sam asked.

The receptionist pointed down the hall.

❧

WHEN SAM ENTERED the emergency room there were two nurses, a doctor, and a maintenance man discussing how long it would take to fix the broken CAT scan machine.

Sam walked up and politely asked the status of Jessica Kealoha.

"Are you her husband?" the doctor asked with a tinge of annoyance in his voice.

"Yes." Sam was going all in.

"I'm Dr. McGee. It's possible she might have a subdural hematoma. She needs a CT Scan to know for sure. Our machine just broke and won't be fixed for at least three days."

"Where's the next closest one?" Sam asked.

The doctor's brow furrowed. "Maui," he said.

Sam reached his right hand up to rub the back of his neck for a minute as he contemplated what to do. Forty-five seconds later he said, "I'll have a chopper here in twenty minutes to take her to the airport. Then I'll have my plane take her to Maui. She should be there in less than an hour. Will that work for you, doc?"

Dr. McGee smiled. "That will work just fine; I'll call Maui Memorial to give them a heads-up on her arrival."

A tad over twenty minutes later, just as Sam said, the Kona fire department helicopter landed on the roof of the hospital. They strapped the gurney with Jessica on to the chopper's skid. The chopper lifted off right away, as if leaving a hot LZ in Iraq.

It was baffling to the hospital staff how Sam could get use of the fire department's helicopter. Nobody could remember it ever being used as an air ambulance in the past.

What they didn't know was Sam Stewart was worth over five billion dollars and could make things happen, with his checkbook, that folks with fewer resources could never imagine.

A phone call to the fire department chief, with the promise of donating a new custom-built rescue boat for the Kona side of the island, was what made magic happen that day.

The fire department chopper landed on the ramp near Sam's jet. Captain Mike Thompson was in the cockpit ready to spin up the engines as soon as they brought Jessica on board. Time was of the essence. The ER doctor said they had a narrow window of time in which to treat her, and the sooner she got to Maui, the better.

Captain Thompson didn't waste any time getting the jet's wheels up and off of the runway. He pushed forward the throttles to full power and the Gulfstream G-6 climbed out of Kona like a rocket heading for space. That day they would find out how fast a sixty million dollar jet could get to Maui from Kona.

Twelve minutes after taking off from Kona, Captain Thompson contacted Maui air traffic control. He declared an emergency, and they gave him priority clearance to land.

A Life Flight helicopter was waiting on the ramp to take Jessica to Maui Memorial and just as Sam said, she was there in less than an hour.

After giving Jessica a CAT scan they wheeled her into the operating room for emergency surgery.

Sam went to the hospital's chapel and prayed that God would save her. *Please, don't take her from me* was his only prayer as his eyes welled up with tears.

5

Sam left voice messages and emailed Uncle Jack and Pua, letting them know that Jessica had been in an accident, was at Maui Memorial and going into surgery soon.

Uncle Jack called Sam from Singapore as soon as the email flashed across the screen of his phone.

"How is she?" he asked.

"The neurosurgeon says he needs to perform a procedure to relieve swelling of the brain. He says the odds are in her favor since she's young and in good health, but other than that he's not saying much."

"I'll be on the next thing smoking back to Hawaii," Uncle Jack said.

As Sam got off the phone with Uncle Jack, Pua finally arrived at the hospital and found Sam in the waiting room. Her eyes were red and puffy. It took her hours to get a flight to Maui because all the earlier flights were booked. With no other choice than to fly standby, she got lucky and caught the last flight out.

Sam and Pua sat in the waiting room and talked about all the good times they had with Jessica.

"You have to promise me you won't tell her I told you this," Pua waited for Sam to acknowledge.

"Okay, I promise."

Pua's face lit up for just a moment, "She was in love with Mighty Mouse when we were kids."

Sam smiled.

"No, you don't understand, she was kissing the TV when he was on. It was *that* kind of love!" They both laughed until they cried over that one. They continued on telling stories to each other about Jessica until they both fell asleep in their chairs at around 1 a.m. waiting for news of her condition.

❧

5 A.M.

The surgeon, Dr. Goldberg, came to the waiting room to give Sam and Pua an update. They had been awake a little while and were drinking coffee, since neither of them could sleep more than a couple of hours.

"Mr. Stewart, the surgery went well and Jessica's prognosis is good. I'm optimistic about her recovery. If there're no complications, she can go home in a couple of days. Your wife is in her room now and you may go see her if you like."

Pua looked at Sam with a raised eyebrow but said nothing.

After Dr. Goldberg left the room Pua remarked, "Your wife, huh?"

Sam glanced at her with a smirk on his face but didn't answer as they continued down the hall toward Jessica's room.

Jessica was asleep when Sam and Pua walked into her room. They wanted to be with her, hug her and maybe hold her hand to make a connection. One they had feared might never happen again.

As Sam stood there on one side of the bed holding her

hand, and Pua on the other side, Jessica's eyes opened slightly. Still heavily sedated, she managed a faint smile and then nodded back out.

☙

THE NEXT DAY Pua had to fly back to Kona. The sale of one of the most expensive properties she had ever sold on the Big Island was getting ready to close escrow. There was a problem between the seller and buyer that wasn't going to fix itself.

The seller was being a jerk about something that the buyer said was a deal breaker. If she wanted the biggest commission check of her career, she had to get back to Kona to fix the deal before it blew up.

While in the waiting room, Sam had taken his last pain pill hours earlier. Sitting there for hours had caused the sciatic nerve in his left leg to radiate a sharp pain all the way down to his ankle. It felt like a knife being jabbed into his lower back. The cherry on top was a knot that had formed in the back of his leg, above the knee, as a result.

After Pua had left, Sam called his doctor to get a pain pill refill. The doctor called it into a twenty four hour pharmacy there on Maui. He told Sam this was the last time he would do so until Sam had surgery to correct the bulging disk in his back.

Sam told Jessica's nurse he'd be back as soon as possible. He then got an Uber to take him to the pharmacy to get his pain pills.

☙

THE FOG of the anesthesia was starting to clear in Jessica's brain as she lay in bed thinking about the accident. She still couldn't fathom why the brakes suddenly wouldn't work in her almost-new Jeep. The nurse interrupted her thought when she came in to take a blood sample. Jessica was starting to think the woman was a vampire with the number of vials she had brought with her to fill with blood.

"Your husband asked me to tell you he'd be right back."

Jessica was still pretty buzzed from the anesthesia. She wondered for a moment if she had gotten drunk, gone to Vegas and gotten married?

"There he is," the nurse said, as Sam walked into the room.

Sam leaned over to hug Jessica and she whispered in his ear, "Did we get married?" She was half kidding and half serious.

He whispered back, "No, honey. I may have misrepresented our relationship with the hospital just a tad so I could see you sooner rather than later." Jessica smiled and lightly squeezed his hand.

⁂

UNCLE JACK ARRIVED at the hospital eighteen hours after hearing from Sam. Since his brother Mike's death, Uncle Jack felt it was important to be there for the family, though he was never a family man himself.

Because Uncle Jack was semi-retired, he had a lot more free time to be around the family. That is, when he wasn't busy running off to Asia on classified government business. Or running fishing charters out at the harbor in Kona.

Jessica was awake and in good spirits, when Uncle Jack lightly knocked on the partially open door, as he walked into her room. He thought she looked like death warmed over with her head bandaged and two black eyes.

"If you think I look bad, you should see the other guy," she cracked, before Uncle Jack had a chance to say anything.

"Well, I see there's nothing wrong with your sense of

humor. I guess I was worried for nothing. I might as well go back to the strip club."

Jessica started to laugh and then stopped. "Don't make me laugh, it makes my head hurt."

Then Uncle Jack got a serious look on his face. "Okay, let's talk about what happened."

"All I know is the brakes wouldn't work, I stepped on the pedal fifty times and nothing happened." Jessica paused for a second. "My Jeep only has about ten thousand miles on it. It doesn't make any sense."

"Maybe it wasn't an accident," Uncle Jack suggested. "Maybe someone wanted you dead?"

Jessica frowned, "I thought about that after the crash. Everybody I put away is on the mainland. I don't have any enemies here that I know of."

They looked at each other and, at almost the same time, they both said, "The EDR needs to be looked at."

"I used to date a mechanic in LA who was an expert witness in a lot of court cases related to vehicle accidents, and he was always talking about the black box in late model vehicles. The Jeep's Event Data Recorder would be the best place to see what the "black box" recorded just before and during the crash. Maybe it would lead to an answer as to why the brakes didn't work."

"Where were you coming from before the crash?" asked Uncle Jack.

"I was coming back from Aloha Village."

"What about one of those dolphin tour companies trying to permanently silence you since you're always writing letters to the editor about how they should be tightly regulated? There's a lot of money to be lost if you succeed in putting them out of business."

"I just want them to quit harassing the dolphins, and disrupting their rest cycle since the long-term effects are most likely harmful to them. Speaking of dolphins, how's Keiki and Koa these days?" Jessica asked.

"I'm sad to say the Navy took them back. They're gearing up in case of war in the Korean peninsula. It's possible I'll get them back someday. They're the best fishing partners I've ever had. I miss them a lot."

Uncle Jack could see Jessica was tired and needed her rest. He told her he was going to Kona to get the EDR out of the Jeep and take it to an automotive technician he knew that could access the data. This guy could tell them whether or not it was sabotage.

6

_____

J ack Murphy knew exactly who to have analyze the data
in the Jeep's black box. Kimo Silvers was the only guy
on the island who had the electronic tools and expertise
to interpret the data. He was a crusty old mechanic turned
technician who lived about fifty miles south of Kona, in an
area called Ocean View.

The one thing Kimo Silvers liked more than fixing cars
was fishing. That's how Uncle Jack knew him. Kimo had chartered Jack's boat the *A Hui Hou* many times to take him fishing. While out fishing they had talked about fixing modern
vehicles on numerous occasions. Kimo told Uncle Jack
modern vehicles were more like computers with four tires
and that mechanics were now called technicians. During
those outings Uncle Jack sensed Kimo felt a lack of respect
from the general public and thought they viewed most technicians as *grease monkeys*.

Uncle Jack drove up the long concrete driveway leading to
Kimo's house. The driveway was spotless. Kimo had been
known to tell people to park at the bottom of it if he knew
their car leaked oil. He didn't want any oil stains on his driveway. And his shop looked more like a sterile environment to

build rockets than an automotive repair shop. The walls were painted white, and the floor shined with a light gray epoxy coating. Along the wall was a large red toolbox filled with every kind of tool a tech would need to fix modern vehicles.

Uncle Jack handed the EDR to Kimo, who placed it on the workbench top of his toolbox and got to work.

Uncle Jack sat on a stool nearby and kept his mouth shut while he watched a master tech at work.

Kimo figured out exactly what happened in less than fifteen minutes, after hooking the EDR to his scan tool and evaluating the data.

"Somebody hacked the onboard computer and turned the brakes off using their laptop," Kimo said.

"Is there any doubt?"

"No. Whoever did this knew what they were doing. They hacked into the anti-lock brake computer using the Jeep's internet connection. Then they shut off the brake fluid at the ABS modulator. It didn't matter how many times she pumped the brake pedal, nothing would happen because the hacker was then in control of the hydraulic fluid that actuated the brakes. His goal was to prevent the brakes from working and he accomplished that goal."

"Is there a way to figure out who did this?" Uncle Jack asked.

"Not from the hack itself, but I'd look at the Jeep for either a GPS tracking device or a camera. Chances are the tracker was custom-built and might have clues that lead you to the hacker. I'd bet dollars to donuts you'll find one or both of them on the vehicle somewhere. The hacker knew the vehicle was going down Kam lll when he turned off the brakes. With a six percent downgrade, it wasn't a fluke he picked that hill to try and kill her on. And, it would like look like an accident."

Uncle Jack thanked Kimo, then went back to the police impound yard and searched the mangled wreckage of the

Jeep. Sure enough, just like Kimo said, there was a GPS tracker. But this tracker was unlike anything Jack Murphy had ever seen before. The tracker also had a wireless router built into it that somehow allowed the hacker to access the Jeep's onboard computer via the internet. It was a sophisticated, custom-built piece of hardware with Russian characters on it. The hacker had hidden it on top of the trailer hitch. Jack never found the camera, but he didn't need to. The tracking device was enough to tell him someone had tried to kill Jessica. Now it was time to get her a bodyguard and find out who wanted her dead.

7

D r. Goldberg released Jessica from the Maui hospital a couple of days after her surgery. She and Sam flew back to Kona that morning. She looked out the window of the jet, after landing, as it taxied to its parking place at the south end of the ramp. That was where all the private jets parked. She saw a black Chevy Suburban waiting nearby with a familiar-looking woman leaning against the side of it. The woman was holding an umbrella to shield her from the intermittent light rain that morning. As the jet got closer to the Suburban, she recognized it was her old friend and former colleague. There was no mistaking her long straight black hair. Like Jessica, Gabbie's parents were different races. Her mother was African American and her father Cherokee Indian. She had light, caramel colored skin and, because of her stunning beauty, had been approached to be a model more than once.

They had been through some tough situations together and formed a lifelong bond like that of veterans who had gone off to war together and survived.

At one time Gabbie and Jessica had become so close that Jessica wanted to become an FBI agent, too. But she failed the background investigation. The Los Angeles Police Department didn't know that Jessica had yakuza gang members in the family. But the FBI did, because of their investigation of the Japanese crime syndicate in Honolulu, and that was a deal breaker for them to hire her.

When Jessica saw Gabbie waiting for her at the bottom of the jet's staircase, both of their eyes lit up with excitement. They hugged after Jessica slowly came down the stairs to the tarmac.

"What are you doing here?" said a surprised Jessica.

"I've come to stay with you until we catch whoever tried to kill you."

Jessica paused for a second. "How did you know?"

"Uncle Jack called me."

Sam was right behind Jessica and had been helping steady her down the stairs.

Jessica introduced them after she and Gabbie hugged again.

"It's nice to finally meet you, Special Agent Harris," Sam said.

"Just call me Gabbie," she replied, as she grabbed Jessica's arm to help steady her as they slowly walked to the Suburban.

"Okay Gabbie. Deal," Sam winked and chuckled.

Jessica looked confused for a moment and then looked at both of them. "You guys know each other?"

Gabbie nodded and was the first to answer. "After Uncle Jack called and filled me in on someone trying to kill you, he put me in touch with Sam. We decided someone should be with you at all times until the perp is found. I thought what better time to come to Hawaii, spend some time with you and help keep you safe while you recover."

Jessica didn't want people to go out of their way for her, but she was too weak to argue about it. After thinking about it for a moment, she decided it would be nice to have an old girlfriend stay with her for a while. Sam had a major business trip in London scheduled that he couldn't cancel and it would be nice to catch up with Gabbie. Otherwise he would have had his own security people protect her. This was going to be better, since she would insist Gabbie stay in the house not only as a bodyguard but as a guest.

Plus, it would be great to reminisce about old times. Except for the Grand Canyon trip. They had agreed the day Gabbie's husband, Karl, fell in the canyon, that they would never discuss what happened that day ever again.

8

J essica had spent the first week home in bed recuperating. On the eighth morning she felt like getting out of bed for the first time since coming home from the hospital. She sat on the couch in her robe and stared at the boats in the bay while waiting for Gabbie to bring her a cup of coffee.

"How are you feeling?" Gabbie handed Jessica her coffee.

"After being washing machined in the Jeep and having my skull drilled into, even my hair hurts today."

The second week after surgery, she was able to go out to the lanai and have her morning coffee. And by the third week she was getting stronger every day. She was starting to feel as though she had enough strength to make the long overdue trip to see Aimee's mother and offer her condolences.

Two days into the third week of her recovery, Jessica asked Gabbie to drive her to Waimea to meet with Mrs. Gaspar.

Earlier that morning, Jessica had called ahead to set a time to meet. Later that afternoon she and Gabbie drove to Mrs. Gaspar's home. They took the high road up over Mt. Hualalai using an armored Chevy Tahoe that Uncle Jack borrowed, and had flown in, until Jessica's assassin could be captured or killed.

On the green rolling hills of Parker Ranch, just outside of Waimea, was the Gaspar ohana. Every day of the previous week the sky had been gray, and the air tasted like sulphur. But that morning a Kona wind came out of the south and blew the volcanic haze towards Maui and Honolulu. It was so clear that day, Jessica pointed out Maui to the northwest and Mauna Kea to the east. She and Gabbie could even see the observatories on top of Mauna Kea at an elevation just shy of thirteen thousand feet, the highest mountain in Hawaii.

Jessica then gave Gabbie a bit of a history lesson as they passed one of the few volcanic cinder cones near the road. A road that she liked to refer to as a two-lane pig trail with asphalt. The cinder cones in the area were similar in size and shape to Mount Suribachi on the Japanese island of Iwo Jima.

"You know the famous picture of the Marines raising the flag during Word War II?" Jessica asked.

Gabbie nodded. "Of course."

Jessica pointed to a cinder cone that was about five hundred feet tall and said, "You see that hill? It was used to train US Marines for the attack on the Japanese at Iwo Jima in 1945."

Gabbie nodded again. "Now, it's green and undisturbed, it looks so peaceful."

"Yes, it does, but to this day the US government is still searching for unexploded ordnance on the land surrounding this area. Because this is where thousands of Marines took part in live fire training during the war."

After Gabbie listened to Jessica describe the area with enthusiasm she said, "If you don't want to go back into police work, maybe you should start a tour company. I almost feel like I've been on a mini tour. You would be a great tour guide."

"I like sharing my knowledge about the island, but I don't

think I want anything to do with working with the public again. On second thought, maybe I might like running a dive boat, then half the time the clientele would be under water and I wouldn't have to listen to them complain about anything until they were back on the boat. And if they got too whiny, I could make them walk the plank!"

Gabbie cut her eyes toward Jessica. "Yeah, you need more time off." And they both laughed.

§

WHEN GABBIE and Jessica arrived at the Gaspar home in Waimea, they could see Aimee's mother sitting in a rocking chair on the lanai waiting for them.

She lived alone, except for her grandson, Henry. Her husband had been a paniolo cowboy for the largest ranch in Waimea for many years before he died of cirrhosis of the liver. Like many families, alcoholism had taken a heavy toll on the Gaspar ohana.

"Aloha, Tutu," Jessica said, as she hugged the smiling woman. "This is my longtime friend, Gabbie."

As Gabbie reached out her hand, the older woman brushed it aside, instead extending her open arms to hug Gabbie.

"Please, my child, call me Tutu… I'm grandmother to all."

And Gabbie learned the real meaning of aloha.

Tutu invited Jessica and Gabbie to sit with her on the lanai and offered them sun tea on ice while they talked.

After a few minutes of pleasantries about the drive to Waimea and the beautiful blue sky, Jessica got right to the point.

"I'm so sorry for your loss," she said while holding the elder woman's hand.

A moment later Jessica heard an excited young boy yell through the front screen door, "Auntie Jessica!"

It was Henry, and he had just woken up from his nap. He was Aimee's son, and the court had placed him with his grandmother Mrs. Gaspar a couple years prior. The judge had appointed her his temporary guardian until Aimee could stay sober and get her life back together.

Henry barreled out of the door and ran to Jessica. He had his little arms stretched out so she could pick him up like she had so many times before. The family court judge had agreed to let Aimee have visitation as long as Jessica was there with her and Henry.

Jessica leaned down and gave Henry a big hug and a kiss on the cheek. She never had any desire for kids, after practically raising her two younger sisters. Their mother had died when Jessica was only twelve. But for some reason she had a soft spot for Henry, that she was feeling more intensely, now that his mother was gone.

Henry sat on Jessica's lap while she and his grandmother talked for a few minutes. Then Tutu said to Henry, "Why don't you take Miss Gabbie in to the kitchen and get some cookies and milk. You know where they are."

"Okay, Tutu," Henry's little voice replied.

Gabbie took the hint and followed Henry inside to the kitchen.

After he was out of earshot, she said to Jessica, "Aimee had a sizable life insurance policy. But the insurance company is trying to get out of paying it on a technicality. I have a lawyer dealing with them, but I'm afraid time will run out before…"

The look on Mrs. Gaspar's face was ominous. Then she continued, "I have stage four breast cancer, and it has metastasized and spread to my brain. I don't know what I will do with Henry. All of my family is gone, and Henry's father is in prison in Arizona. Henry will need that insurance money as he grows up because I won't be here to take care of him."

Tears started to stream down Jessica's cheeks.

Aimee's mom was a tough old woman. "Don't cry for me. Cry for Henry," she said.

Jessica wiped the tears away before Gabbie and Henry returned.

"I'm so sorry to hear that you're sick. I'll do anything I can to help you and Henry. Just tell me what I can do."

With all earnestness Tutu stared into Jessica's eyes. "Would you consider taking Henry?"

Jessica thought for a moment before replying. "I'm not saying no, but because of my head injury, the jury is still out on me for another week or two according to my doctor. What I can do, is make you a promise that no matter what, I will see to it someone takes care of him."

Jessica didn't mention the crash that had killed Aimee wasn't an accident. Or that the man responsible was still on the loose. She thought it wise to make sure he was no longer a threat before making a commitment to adopt Henry. The last thing she wanted to do was put him in danger and make Henry an orphan again. It was bad enough she felt responsible for his mother's death.

When it was time to leave, Jessica hugged Tutu and then picked up Henry and kissed him on the cheek and whispered in his ear, "I'll be back." Then tearfully she set him down and walked to the Tahoe without looking back.

As they stood on the lanai, Tutu held Henry's little hand while they waved aloha to Jessica and Gabbie.

❦

THE FIRST TEN minutes on the way back to Kona it was quiet inside the Tahoe. Then Gabbie asked Jessica, "Have you reconsidered having kids?"

"What makes you ask that?"

"I saw a sparkle in your eyes, when you had Henry on your lap, that I've never seen before."

Jessica smiled for the first time since leaving Waimea. "Henry is such a sweet little boy, I can't help but love him."

"Have you ever thought about having a child with Sam?"

"I'm way too old for that." Then her smile went away.

Gabbie looked at Jessica and said, "First of all, no, you're not. And second, maybe you need one who's going to be all alone out there in the world and who's already potty trained." She turned her eyes back to the road.

"I take it you overheard Tutu?"

"Yeah, I did, while Henry was getting the milk out of the refrigerator."

Jessica said nothing, but Gabbie could see she was thinking about what Gabbie had said earlier, as they drove back to Kona. But first they needed to find out who had tried to kill Jessica–murdered Aimee– and deal with him.

9

I t was dawn. As the sun rose, it made the clouds on the horizon pink and the surface of the ocean had a purple hue.

Gabbie and Jessica sat out on the lanai facing Keauhou Bay while sipping Kona coffee and watching three outrigger canoes paddle out of the bay toward the open sea. There was a light breeze coming off the mountain, flowing toward the ocean. It was 6:30 a.m. and the birds were chirping; sounding the alarm to wake up. A humid scent of rain was in the air from the early morning rain.

Jessica's sworn enemy was a lone rooster, too stupid to tell time, that had been crowing since 4 a.m. He was on her to-do list. Her mission someday would be to find him and ring his neck to eliminate the noise. Not that she really would, but it was a nice thought she entertained from time to time. She had lots of those types of thoughts about people, places, and things that annoyed her, but she didn't act on them. It was a daily struggle for her sometimes, getting along with people, especially the stupid ones.

"This is beautiful, but do you ever get tired of looking at the ocean?" Gabbie asked.

"No, not since I spent twenty-two years working in LA looking at the concrete and asphalt every day. I enjoyed the mainland all I could stand. Don't get me wrong, I'm glad I went there. But I'm happy to be home now that I'm back on the island."

Gabbie smiled and said, "I'm glad to see your taste in men has improved. How did you and Sam meet?"

"After my father's death I came back to Kona to find out what happened and met Sam at Aloha Village. He was a good friend of my father, and one thing led to another. I needed some help on the investigation and he had some unique contacts that I didn't. It was better for me if I collaborated with him. So I did."

"What type of connections are we talking about here?" Gabbie asked.

Jessica took another sip of her coffee before answering.

"The governor of Hawaii, two former US Presidents and other heads of state in various countries. They're all in Sam's phone contact list. At the time I was investigating what happened to my father, Sam had a meeting with the governor at The Ming Resort." Jessica paused to take another sip of her coffee, while Gabbie added more cream and sugar to hers and then continued.

"I wanted to tag along so I could talk to The Ming's CEO Mr. Lau. He had tried to buy Aloha Village from my father and had made multiple low ball offers. My father refused to sell it to him because he knew Lau would ruin the property. The addition to The Ming that Lau wanted to build, would require using Aloha Village's beachfront property, and my father would have died first before allowing that to happen. Up to that point I hadn't been able to get a meeting with Lau, until Sam stepped in," Jessica said.

And then she continued. "That's why he couldn't cancel his trip to Europe. He's got an important meeting with the Prime Minister in London."

"Is he some kind of prince and you're a secret princess?" Gabbie asked half joking.

"Okay, the truth is..." Jessica paused for effect, "he's a nice guy. I like him for who he is, not because he's wealthy. But that doesn't hurt. I used to work at the resorts here on the island when I was a teenager. I met a lot of filthy rich men who wanted me for a play toy. Sam's not like any of them, he's a good guy. He's different from a lot of successful men I've known or dated over the years. He's humble, polite and cares what I think. I wouldn't care if he wasn't wealthy, I'd still be with him."

Gabbie smiled and said, "I'm happy for you. You deserve a prince after some of the guys you were with before."

"Thanks," Jessica smiled.

Gabbie shifted to a serious question. "I know you've focused on Aimee as of late, but we need to talk about the elephant in the room, which is the reason I'm here. Who do you think might want to cause you harm?"

Jessica stirred her coffee with a spoon, while looking down into the mug, and thought about it for a minute before answering.

"I don't have the slightest idea. I've been thinking about what happened since I woke up in the hospital. And whether it was an accident. But Uncle Jack's mechanic guru says someone hacked the computer in my Jeep and turned the brakes off. Uncle Jack also told me he has a friend in the NSA over in Honolulu that's checking airline flights into Hawaii. He's looking at the passenger manifests for the past month to see if any known bad guys have flown into the islands."

Gabbie mused, "What I could do with the internet investigation tools those NSA guys have at their disposal. But since there's still a Bill of Rights, I don't think it's happening in the foreseeable future. I'm almost sure they can read everything transmitted on the internet."

Jessica's tone shifted, she put the palms of her hands up to her cheeks and acted surprised with what was an obvious heavy dose of sarcasm. "You mean they can read all the sexy emails I get from Sam?"

"Yeah, some NSA guy is getting his jollies reading your email," Gabbie answered, and they both laughed.

Jessica's phone on the table next to her started to vibrate. She glanced at it, saw it was Uncle Jack, but let it go to voicemail since she was enjoying her coffee time with Gabbie.

"He'll leave a message if it's important."

A minute later a message icon lit up on her phone.

"I guess it was, I better see what's up. Excuse me for a minute or two."

While Jessica listened to Uncle Jack's voicemail, Gabbie turned in her chair to watch a tour boat a couple hundred yards across the bay. It was loading a herd of pale, white tourists for a day out on the ocean.

Jessica set the phone down and slid back into her lounge chair and let out a sigh.

"I think we have a suspect now," she said.

Gabbie turned back from looking at the tour boat and gave Jessica her undivided attention. "Oh, who?"

"A Russian named Ivan Volkov."

Gabbie looked perplexed. "I don't recognize the name."

"I don't recognize the first name, but I do recall a guy with the last name Volkov I had a bad deal with years ago."

"So the question is, who is this Ivan guy you pissed off enough that he wants you dead?"

"Uncle Jack said he's the brother of an international assassin named Vlad Volkov who is now deceased. I don't know this Ivan Volkov. But I suspect he's got a problem about the bullet I put in his brother's forehead," Jessica said.

"Yeah, that would tend to piss me off if you did that to my brother," Gabbie said, before she started laughing.

Jessica smiled and said, "You should think about seeing someone about the things that make you laugh."

Gabbie then took a serious tone, "Don't you worry, girl, we'll find this piece of crap and take care of business."

Jessica became serious again as she stared at a sailboat entering the bay and said, "Before you came to join the LA Soviet Task Force, Vlad Volkov flew in from Florida to pop a couple of Armenians over in East Hollywood. It was a contract hit because the Armenians screwed a Russian mob guy from Florida who was new in town. The mob wanted to send a message to the Armenians that any transgressions would come with a death sentence. The FBI had Volkov under surveillance when he got off the plane in LA. He was a former KGB agent working his way up to the top of the mob, one murder at a time. They knew he was responsible for half a dozen killings in Florida, but they couldn't tie him to any of them. They told me at the time they suspected he was in town to carry out a hit, but they didn't know who the target was."

Jessica took another sip of her coffee and then sat the mug down on the table between the chaise lounges she and Gabbie were lying on.

"The whole thing went south when Volkov realized he was being tailed and he rabbited. He got away, but two days later the FBI got a break in the case with a tip to the motel where he was hiding out at. They asked us for backup, so we went to his room and it turned into a disaster. The psycho son of a bitch walks up from behind us, as we're getting ready to enter his room, pulls out his piece and starts firing. He had some serious skills."

Jessica paused for a minute, her bottom lip quivering. The memory was still painful for her years later.

"He shot my partner and the two FBI agents we were with in the head before they had time to react. He shot me three times in the back which knocked me down, but I had my bullet-proof vest on under my jacket and I only had the wind knocked out of me." Still haunted by the shooting, she paused again before taking a sip from her water bottle sitting on the table.

"It happened so fast." She looked at Gabbie. "Once he realized I had a vest on he tried to finish me, but his gun jammed. He had it pointed at my head and pulled the trigger. By that time I had my Glock aimed at him. I told him to drop his weapon and freeze. Instead, he acted like he was going to set it down but reached for his backup in an ankle holster. He gave me no choice. I was the only surviving officer out of the four that went to his motel room that morning."

Before either of them said another word, there was a loud knock on the front door.

"Might be Uncle Jack," Jessica said.

Gabbie jumped up. "Sit tight," she said, as she went to see who was at the door. She squeezed Jessica's shoulder lightly as she passed by.

Uncle Jack stood outside the front door and waited for someone to answer. Most days he tapped on the door and walked in. But he didn't want to become an accidental gunshot victim since everyone was on high alert for Ivan Volkov. When Gabbie opened the door she was holding a Glock in her left hand, then quickly stowed it in the holster on her hip.

Uncle Jack glanced at the pistol. "I knew I called the right person," he said.

He went to the kitchen, poured himself a cup of coffee and joined Jessica and Gabbie out on the lanai behind the house.

Jessica was watching a school of yellow tangs hover in the shallow part of the bay near the dock behind the house.

"I never tire of watching them," she said to Uncle Jack as he walked up with a cup of coffee.

While staring at the fish he took a sip and then said, "My source at the NSA said that Ivan Volkov entered the country two weeks ago."

"Okay, any ideas where we find this guy?" Gabbie asked.

Before he could respond, Jessica blurted out "The Ming."

Uncle Jack nodded in agreement. "That was the first place I checked before I called you. If he's staying there, it's under an alias."

Gabbie interrupted. "Why The Ming?"

"When the Chinese triads got run off the island, they sold it to a company controlled by the Russian mob," Uncle Jack said.

"Birds of a feather," Jessica commented.

Uncle Jack reached into his pocket and pulled out a photo and handed it to Gabbie, who looked at it and then handed it to Jessica. "I got it from my contact at the NSA. INTERPOL Canberra has had him on their radar for some time too. He's wanted for hacking two banks in Australia. For him to risk being arrested while traveling internationally, he's got to have some serious desire for revenge."

"That was years ago, why now?" Jessica asked, with Gabbie nodding in agreement.

"He was in prison at the time of his brother's death and didn't get out until six months ago," answered Uncle Jack.

"What was he in for?" asked Jessica.

"Computer hacking," Uncle Jack said before taking the final sip of his coffee. Jessica didn't say anything but continued to watch the tropical fish in the shallows sway back and forth with the tide.

10

J essica, still weak from the surgery, went back inside the house to lie on the couch for a while and think about how she would breach the subject of Henry with Sam. Their rescue dog, a lovable cocker spaniel named Prince, stretched out across her lap. She stroked his back and rubbed his ears while reading the email on her phone.

"Maybe you should think about getting back into law enforcement here on the island," Gabbie said.

"The answer is still no," Jessica answered.

"Don't you miss the camaraderie?"

"I do. But I'm young enough that I'd like to do something else in my life."

"Like what?"

"I'm not sure yet. But I'm starting to want to take you diving and make you walk the plank if you don't stop asking me about going back on the job."

Jessica changed the subject by asking Gabbie a question. "Have you ever gone deep sea fishing?"

"Nope, is this another way for you to make me walk the plank?"

Jessica grinned. "Today's your lucky day, we're going fishing."

Gabbie looked nervous. "What if I get seasick?"

"Well, I guess you'll throw up over the side of the boat. The good news is I doubt you will get sick because the ocean on this side of the island is pretty calm most of the time. The Kona side is protected from the prevailing winds by the five volcanos that make up the island. Mauna Kea and Mauna Loa are the two biggest mountains at over twelve thousand feet tall. They act like giant wind breaks. And besides, what could be safer than being isolated offshore on a boat? Unless of course Ivan Volkov is a part-time pirate or something."

"You do have a point," Gabbie conceded.

Jessica grabbed a tube of sunblock and handed it to Gabbie. "Just make sure you put a lot of this on or you'll get barbecued out on the water."

"So where is this boat we're going to go out on?" Gabbie asked as she looked nervously at the dingy tied up to the dock.

"It's over there." Jessica pointed toward the Cabo 40 fishing yacht moored in the middle of Keauhou Bay.

"Whoa, that's a seriously big boat. You know how to handle one that big?"

"My sisters and I were raised around boats. My dad took us fishing every chance he got. He taught each of us how to handle a boat, catch fish and be all-around good fishermen."

Gabbie continued to rub on sunblock as she listened to Jessica.

"As far as the boat goes, don't worry, you'll love it. It's just like a house inside. Well, actually it's better than some apartments I've lived in. You'll see."

Gabbie and Jessica left the dock in the dingy and cruised out to where the big yacht was moored. As they approached the stern, Gabbie could see the name *Jessica* painted on the back of the boat. Gabbie was sitting in the front of the dingy;

she turned around and gawked with her mouth open at Jessica who was beaming with pride. Jessica said, "What can I say, Sam likes me?" They both laughed.

Gabbie had never been out on the ocean before and the seas were calm that day, just as Jessica had said they would be.

Jessica was feeling just well enough to handle the boat. She fired up the twin eight hundred horsepower diesel engines and told Gabbie how to cast off the mooring lines.

After idling out of Keauhou Bay, Jessica set the autopilot. She rigged a fishing pole to troll as they headed south towards Kealakekua Bay at about eight knots. Just off of Red Hill, Jessica heard the loud whine of fishing reel gears as line quickly spun off of it. Whatever was on the other end of it was big, and trying its best to get away. She looked where the lure had been behind the boat, and all she saw was a hole in the water off of the port side, and then a nano-second later a huge blue marlin rocketed out of the ocean six to eight feet in the air.

The blue marlin was violently twisting and trying to free itself from the hook that was embedded in its jaw.

Jessica put the boat's transmission into neutral and climbed down as quick as she could from the flying bridge. She grabbed the pole off the back of the transom and pointed Gabbie toward the fighting chair. Since the boat was no longer underway, it started to rock in sync with the light swell that day as Jessica helped Gabbie get to the fighting chair.

"You're going to sit in the chair and reel that monster in, okay?"

"Me?" Gabbie questioned. The uncertainty in her voice was clear.

"Yes, you. I can't fight the fish, I'm too weak from surgery, remember? You're going to have to do it."

Gabbie was reluctant, but accepted the fear. She sat in the fighting chair and reached for the pole.

Jessica thought to herself that they had a slim chance of catching that fish with a rookie handling the pole, but it was worth a try. She would soon realize that she couldn't have been more wrong about Gabbie.

Jessica estimated the weight of the marlin at over five hundred pounds when the big fish first leapt out of the water. What she didn't guess was Gabbie Harris being a natural when it came to big game fishing. For a woman who had never fished one time in her whole life, Gabbie took to it like a dog going after a bone.

After battling the monster-sized fish for close to an hour she asked Jessica a question.

"What are we going to do after we get this thing next to the boat?"

"We're going to tag and release it."

"You mean after I spent all this time reeling this monster in you want to let it go?" Gabbie's eyebrows narrowed.

"Fix your face, that's exactly what I mean. Don't worry, we'll probably catch another fish on the way back that we can have for dinner."

Most of the time when Jessica went out she usually caught an ono or mahi-mahi, but not always.

After she explained the conservation effort behind tagging and releasing the marlin, Gabbie was reluctant to get onboard with the idea, but eventually agreed it was the right thing to do.

"If we tag and release the fish, it has a chance of reaching its full size. They get to over a thousand pounds. Then it becomes what's known as a grander. Some people don't understand you can't just take, take, take from the ocean, or one day there won't be anything left to take."

Gabbie nodded and continued to reel the big fish toward the back of the boat while occasionally giving Jessica a dirty look. That went on for another thirty-two minutes before the magnificent creature was alongside the Cabo.

Just as Jessica predicted, after releasing the Marlin they caught a couple of thirty-pound ono on the way back to Keauhou Bay. Jessica cleaned, filleted, and then grilled the fresh fish that night for dinner. The blue marlin wasn't the only one hooked on that trip. Gabbie Harris was ready to go fishing again the next day. But that would have to wait until Ivan Volkov was in custody or dead, whichever came first.

11

Larry Black was a Kona real estate magnate from Toronto. Or at least that's what he told everyone. He ran a one-stop shop for Russian mobsters who needed to launder millions of dollars. Larry was the go-to guy when it came to ocean front homes, exotic cars, and super yachts. He specialized in the sales of all three. It was nothing for him to put together package deals for his clients that ran into the hundreds of millions of dollars. For the last couple of years Larry Black Ocean Front Realty had been under investigation by the IRS and FBI. But the feds could never find enough evidence to make anything stick.

He was early sixties, tanned, his long silver hair pulled back tight into a ponytail, and he had the physique of a guy who trained for triathlons. He looked like a man much younger than his chronological age. The truth of the matter was that he'd never trained a day in his life. It was because of good genes and human growth hormone that he looked the way he did.

His piercing, ice-blue eyes gave the impression of a man well-traveled who had seen a lot of things in his life. Some good, some bad.

The Russian mob had worked to get a foothold in Hawaii for a few years. There was a small contingent of them living on the Big Island, lying low, operating below the radar. Money laundering was their crime of choice and Larry was their guy.

Nobody in Hawaii cared where the Russian's money came from. Just as long as they had enough of it to buy multi-million-dollar real estate that had been on the market for years during the great recession. They paid cash and never haggled over the price. There had been whispers in the real estate community, but nobody wanted to rock the boat. Why would they since they were all getting rich.

Larry had also sold Uncle Jack the *A Hui Hou* after Sam and Jessica had introduced them during a billfish tournament after-party.

Jessica's attempted murder had been on the six o'clock news for the last two weeks. And Ivan Volkov's photo splattered across the TV screen every night during the newscast. Uncle Jack made sure the TV news director at Channel 8 kept the story front and center every night. He did so by giving the director and his staff a couple of full-day charters out of Honokohau harbor on the *A Hui Hou*.

Each night after the newscast there were plenty of tips that came in with possible sightings. The Kona cops had been chasing them down and, along with Uncle Jack, they were working day and night to find Ivan Volkov, to no avail.

Larry had been watching the nightly news and called Uncle Jack one night after the newscast. He asked him if he had any solid leads yet as to the whereabouts of Ivan Volkov. And that he had a proposal for Uncle Jack.

Larry said, "If you find him before the cops do, I know some people that would be happy to exchange a large cash reward for him. He'll never be a problem to your family again."

"As much as I would like to oblige, I can't do that. In this country people are still entitled to a trial by their peers. Larry, you know you're talking to a retired federal agent, right? I'm going to pretend we didn't have this conversation," and Uncle Jack hung up the phone.

It just wasn't how Uncle Jack did business. No, Ivan Volkov would have to stand trial and go to prison if convicted. And then the Russians could do whatever they wanted with him after he got out, if they could find him.

Larry wasn't stupid, he knew Uncle Jack was retired and there wasn't anything he could do about offering him a bribe for Volkov. He also knew his silent partner would not be happy about the unwillingness of Uncle Jack to turn over Volkov.

12

U ncle Jack was serious about his responsibility of watching over the Murphy ohana since his brother Mike's death.

He wanted Jessica to stay out at Aloha Village until Ivan Volkov could be found or determined to no longer be on the island.

After Jessica listened to Uncle Jack's request, she took a moment before answering. Then she offered a counter-proposal.

"Tell you what, how about Gabbie and I stay on board the Cabo and we'll moor it in Kailua Bay. Would that work for you? We could tie up alongside of the *A Hui Hou* if that makes you feel better."

Uncle Jack wasn't crazy about the idea, but thought it was a reasonable compromise.

"Okay, but you stay on the boat until we catch Volkov," he said.

"Deal," agreed Jessica.

That afternoon Jessica slowly motored the Cabo out of Keauhou Bay, and cruised six miles up the coast to Kailua Bay. When Gabbie and Jessica awoke the next morning, they noticed there was a sixty-five-foot Coast Guard cutter just off the starboard side between them and the pier. Moored on the port side was a super yacht, complete with a helicopter deck named the *Akula*. It was built by Sam's boatyard for a Russian oligarch who was a client of Larry Black's.

As with most small towns, the rumors were flying as to who the owner of the *Akula* was. There was even one going around that said Vladimir Putin owned it.

Nobody knew for sure except Larry Black. And he wasn't talking, since he signed a non-disclosure agreement. It was standard procedure when representing famous clients, or in this case... mobsters.

It looked like Uncle Jack had been busy calling in a favor. It wasn't unusual to see the Coast Guard cutter in Kailua Bay. What was unusual was the fact that the cutter didn't leave the bay during the next three days. As long as Jessica and the Cabo sat in the bay, so did the cutter.

⚓

JESSICA WAS LYING on the couch in the saloon of the Cabo reading a book when her phone rang. She hoped it was good news when she saw it was Uncle Jack. After three days of being moored in Kailua Bay, she was tired of being on the boat and looking at Kailua Village from two hundred yards away.

"Ivan Volkov has problems with the Russians," Uncle Jack said.

Jessica put the phone on speaker; she and Gabbie listened intently to Uncle Jack give them the rundown about what he was doing to find Volkov.

Jessica asked, "What does the Russian government want with him?"

"He wishes the Russian government wanted him. It turns out those banks he hacked were in Australia and both of them belonged to a group of Russian mobsters. A plane with a half dozen of them landed at the Kona airport four hours ago. I doubt they're here to work on their tan. My friend at Homeland Security notified me as soon as the Russian's plane entered US airspace."

Jessica thanked Uncle Jack for the update and told him Sam would be back from London soon, and when he was, she was going home. The Cabo was nice, but it was feeling cramped after three days.

That evening Jessica got a text from Sam.

"Hi honey, just landed, heading home."

Sam's timing couldn't have been better. Jessica wanted to go home and sleep in her own bed. She loved the big boat, but she loved her own bed more.

She started the engines as Gabbie cast off the bow line and they cruised back to Keauhou Bay that night.

&.

It was about 11 p.m. whey they entered Keauhou Bay. There was a light warm rain as Jessica and Gabbie moored the yacht.

Sam was standing at the edge of the dock waiting for them. As the dingy neared the dock he reached out to grab the bow line from Gabbie. Jessica noticed Sam wincing as he reached for the rope. He didn't say anything, but it was clear his back was bothering him again.

After Sam tied the bow line around a cleat on the dock, he extended a hand to help Gabbie and Jessica out of the small boat. As he pulled Jessica onto the doc, he grimaced, but this time he also yelped like a dog in pain. The ongoing back pain resulted from a failed back surgery.

"I'm sorry you're in pain, honey," Jessica said, with a look of sincere compassion on her face.

Sam grimaced and said, "Thanks. Uncle Jack's inside the

house. He swept the place to make sure it was safe. Now he's on the phone talking with his connection down at the Kona PD."

Uncle Jack was standing in the doorway of the sliding glass doors at the back of the house. He watched the trio approach as he was talking on the phone.

"Okay, that's great news, thanks for the phone call, Captain." Uncle Jack clicked off the phone and put it back in his aloha shirt pocket.

"Good news," Uncle Jack said as he looked at Jessica.

"The Kona cops have Ivan Volkov in custody. Apparently he got drunk down at one of the oceanfront bars last night and got his ass kicked by some local guy. Then the cops hauled him and the winner off to jail. When they ran him for warrants they realized who he was. The list of the agencies that want this guy is almost a record, from what the captain said."

Sam was arching his back, like he was trying to get a kink out of it and said, "What does that mean?"

Uncle Jack continued, "Homeland Security has dibs on him first. They'll be over in the morning to pick him up, according to the captain."

Gabbie was the first to respond. "Why do I have the feeling this guy is never going to be seen again."

"We can only hope," Sam said. Jessica nodded and Uncle Jack agreed and said, "I'll drink to that."

Everyone went to bed that night with the satisfaction that it was finally over.

13

I t was just like the captain at the Kona PD said it would be. Two Homeland Security Investigations agents arrived at the police department the next morning and took Ivan Volkov into their custody.

What was waiting for them was something they didn't expect after they left the Kona cell block, a half dozen ex-KGB Agents who had turned mobster. After the fall of the Soviet Union that was the chosen career path of many former KGB.

The HSI agents were driving 25 mph on the airport access road as they approached the rental car road. A large SUV pulled out in front of them, blocking them. The agent driving had to slam on the brakes to keep from crashing into the SUV. Tires screeched from behind, as a minivan skidded up to their rear bumper. Six guys with Kalashnikov assault rifles surrounded the vehicle, black ski masks covered their faces.

"Give him to us and you go home to your families," a man said in broken English, with a Russian accent. He and the others pointed rifles at the agents and Volkov, who was in the back seat of the car.

Both HSI agents agreed they had no plans to die over some Russian hacker. They kept their hands in the air as the ex-KGB team pulled Ivan Volkov out of the backseat and hustled him away to the waiting SUV. The Russians confiscated the phones and guns of the two agents, then slashed their tires so they wouldn't be able to follow them.

It was a well-planned, precision operation to abduct Ivan Volkov. He had their money, and they were going to get it back one body part at a time, if that's what it took. If he was lucky, they would kill him quickly after he returned the money he stole from their bank in Australia.

❧

THE GULFSTREAM JET owned by the Russians flew out of Kona six minutes after they abducted Ivan Volkov from HSI.

It didn't take Homeland Security long to figure out who grabbed Volkov. They called Hickham Air Force Base, and within thirty minutes there was an F-22 Raptor on each wing of the Gulfstream jet a hundred and fifty miles south of the Big Island. *Turn around and return to Honolulu* was the message received loud and clear. The Gulfstream G-6 turned back toward Oahu.

Homeland Security agents boarded the jet at Hickham Air Force Base and the only thing they found was a case of vodka and the two pilots.

By 11:30 a.m., Uncle Jack had heard what happened that morning. He called Jessica. "You ain't gonna believe this shit," Uncle Jack said. He then told her what had happened that morning with Volkov being abducted at gunpoint.

Uncle Jack continued, "There is an upside to this. He'll most likely be dead within twenty-four hours, if he isn't already."

"I hope they sashimi his ass and feed him to the sharks," Jessica said.

"But here's the thing, if he wasn't on the jet that left Kona right after the abduction, where did they take him?" Uncle Jack questioned.

Jessica had been watching a helicopter take off and land on the super yacht *Akula* in Kailua Bay for a couple of days prior, when she and Gabbie stayed there on the *Jessica* .

"Knowing Larry Black, I'd bet my last dollar Volkov is on the *Akula* heading towards Australia. Larry sold that yacht to a Russian oligarch who's been flying off and on it all week with a helicopter," Jessica mused.

"I know what you're thinking. They flew him to the yacht. The Gulfstream was just a diversion," Uncle Jack said.

"I hope that's the end of it with him," Jessica said.

"I could call the Coast Guard to intercept the *Akula* and search it for Volkov if you want," Uncle Jack said.

"Nope, I'm good with the Russians taking care of him. I have enough things I have to worry about. Him getting out of prison and trying to off me again is just something I'd rather not have to think about. Besides, that bastard killed my friend Aimee and now a four-year-old boy is without his mother because of him. So yeah, let the Russians have him."

While Jessica was okay with the Russians taking care of Ivan Volkov, Uncle Jack was not. But he let it go this one time for her. And Larry Black had earned himself a spot on Uncle Jack's shit list. Someday Jack Murphy would peel back the covers of Larry Black's business to see who he was in bed with.

14

It had been over a month since Jessica had surgery and she was well on her way to a full recovery. Dr. Goldberg gave her a clean bill of health after her last checkup.

Sam and Jessica's Keauhou Bay house had a living room with custom-built doors that retracted to open up a forty-foot-wide view of the bay. Cool breezes and the sound of the ocean circulated throughout the house.

It was a cool, crisp morning around 7 a.m., and Jessica had opened the doors and let Prince out to go take care of his business. She and Gabbie were sitting on the couch in the living room facing the bay taking in the view. They drank coffee and watched a couple of beginner stand-up paddle boarders struggle to keep from falling off their boards.

Later that morning they looked at photos in Jessica's scrapbook while reminiscing about old times when they had worked together in LA. Then they looked at some photos Gabbie had taken there on the island.

Protecting Jessica had been Gabbie's number one priority. She had never been to Hawaii before and found its beauty mesmerizing. She couldn't help but take a lot of photos along the way.

Gabbie had taken photos of the *Akula* when it was in Kailua Bay. She was looking at some of them on her iPad and noticed the name on the back of the yacht and asked Jessica what it meant.

"What does *Akula* mean in Hawaiian?"

"It's not Hawaiian. It's Russian. It means shark."

"I didn't know you knew Russian."

"I don't. I know Google."

The women clanked their coffee cups together and laughed.

Then Jessica continued, "I knew it wasn't Hawaiian when I saw it the first day it was here so I googled it."

Being around Gabbie had brought back a lot of old memories that up to this point Jessica had avoided talking about, but felt compelled to inquire about before Gabbie left to go back to the mainland.

"How's your love life? Have you had any men try to put their hands on you since Karl?"

Gabbie shook her head.

"Nope. After Karl I told a couple of guys I dated that I carried a 9mm at all times. I also told them if they ever laid a hand on me in a harmful way, I'd blow their head off."

Jessica felt the tension in Gabbie's voice, knew she wasn't kidding, and decided asking about Gabbie's love life maybe wasn't a good idea. But she was glad Gabbie would never allow herself to become a victim again.

"I swore to myself after Karl that I would never let that happen to me again. The abuse started out gradual and progressed. It's not like I went on a date with him and he beat me and I said let's get married. That's not how it works..."

Gabbie reigned in the seriousness in her tone of voice. Jokingly she said, "I considered becoming a lesbian but the thought of some bitch sharing my closet and borrowing my clothes without asking was just too much."

Jessica just about fell off the couch from laughing so hard. She had missed Gabbie's great sense of humor.

Gabbie took a sip of her coffee and then continued, "I decided to get a dog instead."

Jessica loved dogs and perked up. "What kind?"

"A German Shepherd. His name is Rex, he's a sweetheart. Unless of course you're trying to break into the house, then he'll eat you, since I don't feed him very much. He's much better than any man I ever lived with." Gabbie beamed like a proud parent and pulled up a photo of him on her phone to show Jessica.

"What do I have to do to bring him to Hawaii? I heard it's a huge pain in the ass to bring a dog here," Gabbie asked.

"Because there's no rabies in Hawaii, the state requires a lot of hoops for you and Rex to jump through before they would allow him to come here. Why would you ask?"

"After being here the first week I felt like I was home for the first time. I know that probably sounds weird but I can feel that thing you call "mana" here, like no other place in the world. I'm going to put in my papers and retire. I've asked Pua to find me a house here."

Jessica wasn't sure that would be a good thing. She had changed all her friends on the mainland when she quit drinking and that included Gabbie, too.

Besides being a former colleague, Gabbie was an old drinking buddy. And while they had a lot of good times together drinking, Gabbie reminded Jessica a lot of the times that weren't so great. Like waking up next to 'it' one too many times after a night of hard drinking. Jessica never wanted to feel that way again. Remorse, shame, and self-hatred were old friends that she had broken up with. She had no desire to repeat the past behavior, and felt apprehensive about Gabbie moving to the island.

While Jessica was grateful for Gabbie's help the past few weeks, she was afraid of what could happen if Gabbie moved to Kona. Even though she had been sober a few years, Jessica was cautious about falling into old behaviors that could lead back to the bottle.

"One reason I want to move here is so I can fish. You know you can't fish for marlin in LA. And the other reason is I think you and I should start our own private investigation firm."

Jessica almost spit her coffee out when Gabbie said that. But she choked it down and continued to listen while wondering if Gabbie had gone bat shit crazy from the heat and humidity.

"I don't know, Gabbie. I haven't talked to Sam yet about Henry; I want us to adopt him."

Gabbie smiled.

"That would be great. I hope he agrees; I think you would be a great mother."

Jessica didn't look as happy about it as Gabbie did.

"The thought of being responsible for a kid scares the hell out of me. But I feel responsible for the loss of his mother and can't let him get put into the foster home system."

Gabbie scooted closer, put her hand on top of Jessica's and said, "It's not your fault. Life is a series of choices we make, and sometimes bad things happen as a result of those choices. Good stuff happens and bad stuff happens. It's that simple."

"Okay, Dr. Gabbie. Maybe you should hang out your shingle and be a shrink here instead. Lord knows there's an overabundance of crazy people living on this rock."

Then Jessica said something that stunned both herself and Gabbie.

"How about we call our firm J & G Investigations? We can take photos of cheating bastards and their hussies. Lord knows there's no shortage of them."

Gabbie smiled and nodded she would like that.

THAT NIGHT SAM and Jessica took Gabbie to a luau at Aloha Village. The pig had been in the imu all day, and after dinner Gabbie said it was the most tender and delicious pork she had ever eaten.

The highlight of the evening, besides the food, was the fire knife dancer throwing his flaming stick in the air and catching it. The spinning circles of fire in both of his hands mesmerized the audience.

Later that evening, on the way home from the luau, Sam and Jessica dropped Gabbie off at the airport to catch the red-eye back to the mainland.

When they got home, Jessica said the one sentence that strikes more fear in a man than anything else. "Honey, we have to talk."

"Can it wait until morning? My back is killing me; I need to take a pain pill and lie down."

Jessica sensed he was stalling but agreed to postpone talking about Henry until the morning.

15

The next morning Jessica was making coffee in the kitchen and planned to talk with Sam about Henry. But before she could, Sam kissed her on the cheek and ran out the door saying there was some kind of emergency down at the boatyard. His parting words were, "I love you, we'll talk tonight."

Jessica looked at Sam and nodded.

As he drove to the yard, he figured he bought some time and had better get his plan together before he returned home.

On his way to the boatyard Sam stopped off at the jewelers near the banyan tree downtown.

The jeweler had just opened the shop when Sam walked in. Twenty-five minutes later he walked out with a beautiful diamond engagement ring.

Their lives had been hectic since the attempt on Jessica's life. Sam had not forgotten the promise he had made to himself at the Maui hospital, that he would ask Jessica to marry him if she didn't die. All he could think about was *now she wants to talk*.

That afternoon on the way home he called her. "Hi, honey. How about I pick up a couple of barbecue chicken plates from

L&L Drive-In. We can watch the sunset while cruising up the coast in the Cabo this evening."

"That sounds great, honey. And we can talk about that thing I mentioned last night," she answered.

The knot in Sam's gut grew tighter by the minute just thinking about what she wanted to talk about. But at least she was still calling him *honey.*

His back was killing him from all the tension.

He took a pain pill and in about eight minutes all was right in his world again. Except for the fact that the time between pills was getting shorter and shorter, and their pain relief was less and less.

❦

JESSICA THOUGHT SHARING a sunset together was a great idea and would be the perfect time to broach the subject of Henry.

They had never talked about having kids. Both were in their early forties and thought that ship had sailed a long time ago in their lives.

That evening as they cruised along the coastline it was a little after dusk and the sky had turned from burnt orange with streaks of red and yellow to a solid purple. It was just dark enough that Venus could be seen rising in the west. It had been a perfect sunset minutes earlier and now the lights, on the houses along the coast, were starting to twinkle as the sky grew darker.

Sam had set the autopilot at a leisurely pace of eight knots. The wind was light and warm. They were both sitting on the bridge high above the cockpit and fighting chair. Jessica was rubbing Sam's low back with one hand as he fiddled with the switch for the navigation lights.

"You remember Aimee's little boy, Henry?"

"Sure, he's a sweet kid."

Jessica continued to rub Sam's back as she talked.

"This is what I've been wanting to talk with you about."

Sam had a sigh of relief inside. He had listened to the voices in his head all day, that said she wanted to leave him. Luckily the other guy living in his head that day was wrong.

"Henry's grandmother, Mrs. Gaspar, has stage four breast cancer that has spread to her brain and she only has a few months left to live. There's not going to be anyone left in the family to take care of Henry except his father. And he's in the Arizona State Prison doing fifteen to life."

Sam looked puzzled but focused on every word she said. So far none of them were "I need time alone" that every guy knows is code for *the party's over*.

"I want you to think about Henry coming to live with us." Sam looked like a deer in the headlights and for once was at a loss for words.

The only thing he could muster at the moment was, "Us raise a four-year-old? Is that what you're saying?"

"That's exactly what I'm saying," she answered.

There were a hundred other things that he thought Jessica might want to talk to him about besides breaking up, but adopting a child wasn't on the list. Running a multi-billion-dollar company and being responsible for thousands of jobs didn't bother him. But dealing with an unruly four-year-old scared the crap out of him.

As they were starting to get to the meat of the conversation the wind was starting to blow hard and the weather was changing fast.

Sam turned the boat back toward Keauhou Bay as the surprise squall quickly blew in from the south. Flashes of lightening began to appear on the horizon and the sound of thunder rumbled in the distance.

Within ten minutes the time between the lightning strikes hitting the surface of the ocean and the crackling boom of thunder was getting closer together.

"We can continue this discussion later. You should go

down below and stay inside until we get back to Keauhou or
this storm dies down," Sam said, as the thunder boomed just
a second after the last lightning strike less than a mile away.

Jessica agreed it was the right thing to do and didn't waste
any time getting down off the bridge and going inside the
saloon.

After she was safely below, Sam applied full throttle to the
eight hundred horsepower MAN engines. With the wind
blowing rain sideways in his face, as they raced back to
Keauhou Bay, all he could think about was that Jessica was
the most important person in the world to him. And if she
wanted Henry to come live with them, then he would have to
get on board with the idea or risk losing her, and that was
unacceptable to him. Maybe it wouldn't be so bad. If Jessica
loved Henry, he would, too.

That night after getting back to Keauhou Bay and securing
the Cabo, Sam and Jessica stood in the kitchen looking at each
other. He was leaning against the granite counter while she
was making herself a bowl of cereal. Sam walked over to her
before she could pick the bowl up; he held her in his arms
and kissed the top of her head. Earlier on the boat he knew
his reply about Henry was less than she had hoped for. To get
back on track he looked down at her and said, "Why don't
you tell Mrs. Gaspar that she doesn't have to worry about
Henry. We'll take care of him."

"Are you sure?" she asked, while looking up into his eyes
checking for any sign of wavering.

Sam nodded. "I'm sure."

16

They locked Ivan Volkov in a stateroom on board the *Akula*. His whole right hand was throbbing with pain. So far he was missing only the tip of his pinky finger after the first interrogation. He knew if he told his captors what they wanted to hear he'd be dead shortly thereafter. But them torturing him until he broke wasn't a viable plan either.

"Tell you what, Volkov, you give us our money back and we'll kill you quickly with a bullet in the back of the head," Viktor Zinchenko smirked.

"I'm sorry, I didn't know it was your guys' bank or I would have picked a different one."

"It's too late for that."

Zinchenko set a laptop down in front of Volkov and said, "Return our money or the next thing I will do is cut off your ear."

"Of course I'm going to give you your money back, but I have an offer for you."

Zinchenko slapped Volkov upside the head and screamed, "You idiot, you're in no position to negotiate!"

Zinchenko looked at one of his lieutenants, Nikita Gorev,

and said, "Take this dumbass topside and chop his hands off for stealing and throw him overboard to the sharks."

"Wait!" Volkov cried. He flipped open the laptop and quickly started typing in the browser. Zinchenko raised his hand to stop Gorev.

Ivan transferred back the money he stole plus an extra hundred grand into Zinchenko's bank.

Zinchenko looked at Gorev, "Chop his hands off anyway and let the sharks have him."

Before Gorev could grab him Volkov blurted out, "That's not your money! I hacked another bank besides yours and I just put their money into your account. It's more than you had, check the numbers."

Once again Zinchenko waved off Gorev and proceeded to verify that Volkov had indeed put back more than he had taken. Zinchenko said, "Okay, I'm listening."

Volkov continued. "If you let me live, I can hack a lot of banks for you. I'll make you ten times richer than you already are."

"And you'll still be alive," Zinchenko said.

❧

GOLD COAST, Australia

The Russian mobsters took Ivan Volkov up on his proposition. He was being held in a mansion in Gold Coast, and went to work hacking banks for his captors. He stole more money for them, in a short amount of time, than they had ever dreamt possible.

What he didn't tell his new business partners was that he was good at breaking into banks online, just not good at evading detection. After a rash of online bank robberies in Australia and New Zealand, the Australian Federal Police sought help from the FBI Cyber Action Team, known as CAT. The CAT team flew to Australia within forty-eight hours of the Australians calling and requesting their help. The sole purpose of the CAT team was to track down who was hacking all those banks and stop it.

Volkov made a crucial error on one break-in and didn't realize he had exposed his computer's IP address during the hack. The CAT team traced the IP to the mansion in Gold Coast and the Australian Federal Police raided the compound the next day.

The police arrested Viktor Zinchenko and his crew that were in the mansion at the time. But they overlooked Ivan Volkov, who was in a hidden safe room planning the next heist, when the police busted down the front door.

Volkov heard the police yelling to get down on the floor at everyone. He turned off his computer and sat in the room as quiet as a mouse, for two hours until the cops left. After he was sure, he walked right out the front door and hopped on the AirTrain to the Brisbane airport. Once there, he boarded the first flight to Honolulu to take care of some unfinished business.

17

Sam and Jessica completed the adoption paperwork before Mrs. Gaspar passed away. They had Henry's room all ready with a race car bed frame and all the toys a kid could ever want.

Adopting a soon to be five-year-old boy was a scary proposition. Being responsible for him felt more daunting than anything either of them had tackled before in their lives.

It was the first Saturday morning that Henry had been in his new home, and he seemed to be adapting well. Sam and Henry sat at the breakfast table in the dining room; each eyeballed the other for the first five minutes or so.

A little while later Henry was eating Cheerios and Sam was drinking coffee while reading the morning newspaper. Jessica was in the kitchen trying not to burn the waffles.

Sam looked over the top of his paper at Henry when he felt the little eyes staring at him from the other side of the cereal bowl. Sam folded the newspaper and laid it on the table as Jessica set down a plate full of burnt waffles.

"What would you like to do today, Henry?" Sam asked. Henry shrugged his shoulders. Jessica was busy covering the waffles with butter and syrup, trying to hide her skills of mass destruction when it came to cooking.

Smiling, Sam looked at Henry. "I think today we should go fishing. Have you ever been fishing before?" Henry shook his head no and continued to crunch on a mouthful of Cheerios.

"Okay, that settles it. By the end of today, Henry, you will have caught a fish and piloted a boat," Sam promised. Henry smiled and rapidly nodded yes.

"Just us boys today, honey," Sam said.

"That will be great. I have a book I want to read out on the lanai today. You boys go have fun."

Sam and Henry finished breakfast and then took the dingy out to the Cabo moored in the bay. They headed south out of the bay and trolled using a stinger fishing pole off the bridge. That way Sam could have Henry sit on his lap reeling in a fish and he could still control the boat from there.

Sam wasn't sure what to expect with his first outing alone with Henry, but it went better than he thought it would. Henry was a well-behaved little boy and was easy to be around. Sam had been apprehensive at the thought of adopting him when Jessica first broached the subject.

But he had made a commitment to both Jessica and Henry and vowed he would honor it.

The more time Sam spent with Henry the more he realized the little guy was a blessing for him and Jessica.

The loud whine of the fishing reel gears broke the silence of the sea as it started spinning hundreds of revolutions per minute. At least fifty yards of line peeled off before Sam could get Henry and the fishing pole in a comfortable position on his lap.

"Okay, Henry, put your hand on mine and we're going to work together to reel the fish in. Okay?"

Sam was hoping to catch something like a twenty-pound

ono and not a five-hundred-pound marlin. Catching a small fish would be fun. A big fish would be work.

After they reeled in what Sam estimated was about a forty-pound mahi-mahi, he turned the boat around and headed back home to Keauhou Bay. While cruising back he let Henry sit on his lap and steer the boat.

Before putting the fish on ice, he took a selfie of him and Henry standing at the transom of the boat, holding up the tail of the green and gold shimmering mahi-mahi. Later that night, when he showed Jessica the photo of him and Henry with their catch, he felt satisfaction unrelated to a monetary gain, for the first time in his life. Now if Sam could make it through a party they were scheduled to attend the next day, then being a parent might be easier than he thought it would be.

18

The next day Sam and Jessica took Henry to a birthday party at Spencer Beach Park. The child having the party belonged to a well-liked employee of Sam's boatyard and there was no way he and Jessica couldn't attend.

Jessica warned Sam that it was a first birthday party and it would be bigger than he might expect. That was an understatement.

There must have been a hundred and fifty people there. Sam had never seen anything like it. Jessica explained that ancient Hawaiian babies rarely made it to their first birthday, so when they did, it was a reason to have a big celebration.

When Sam and Jessica arrived with Henry at the party, Pua was already there and sitting at a picnic table. She was talking to a guy ten or fifteen years younger who was probably hoping to catch a cougar that day. After a few minutes of Jessica giving him the stink-eye, he took the hint and wandered off to pursue other opportunities.

A group of kids were playing nearby that were close in age to Henry and they asked if he could play with them.

Jessica said, "Okay, but stay where I can see you." Henry nodded and ran over to play with the other kids.

Pua commented, "He's a quiet little boy."

"He's had a lot of big changes. I suspect once he gets used to us we won't be able to keep him quiet," Jessica said.

The guests that day were a regular who's who from Kona town. Everyone was there. People who Jessica hadn't seen in over twenty years showed up.

Sam and Jessica were sitting at the table with Pua *talking story* of life in general and how Kona's population was growing faster than the infrastructure. They lamented about how the traffic crawled along at a snail's pace compared to the old days.

Jessica had been keeping an eye on Henry while he played with the other kids, and he seemed to be having a good time. Pua noticed Jessica watching him. "It's so sad about his mother and grandmother. But it's great you guys adopted him."

Jessica was getting ready to reply to Pua, but her sister was having one of her manic moments and continued, "I almost forgot, you have to see the photos of my new puppy. He's a French bulldog and is so adorable."

As Pua was thumbing through the photos on her phone Jessica glanced over at Sam and rolled her eyes. Sam mouthed "be nice."

"There he is." Pua held up her phone to show off her "new baby" as she referred to him.

Sam and Jessica were looking at Pua's photos of her baby. It couldn't have been more than a brief moment when Sam looked up to check on Henry.

Sam hopped up from the table to go look for Henry as he tapped Jessica on the shoulder. "I don't see Henry," he said urgently.

When Jessica saw how Sam reacted quickly to not seeing Henry, she felt a moment of relief because she initially wasn't sure how committed to Henry Sam was. His actions spoke loud and clear that he truly cared about Henry, even though it had only been a short period of time that they had been around each other.

In the back of her mind Jessica knew statistically child abductions were rare. Her brain told her Henry probably ran off to go to the bathroom or something, but her gut instinct felt something wasn't right this time.

When it became clear that Henry was missing, Jessica rounded up all the kids he was playing with and asked them if they had seen where Henry went. Or had they seen him walk off with an adult.

None of the kids saw anyone approach Henry. But what they did see was Henry did in fact wander off to the bathroom about a hundred and fifty yards away from where they were playing.

That gnawing in her gut earlier, that something wasn't right, had disappeared and was replaced by the sharpest kind of pang. It felt like a knife in the belly. She had never felt anything like it before.

They put an Amber alert out island wide for Henry. Sam and Jessica stayed at Spencer Beach Park throughout the night looking for him. He had vanished without a trace. At 3 a.m. they went home to wait by the phone and get some much-needed sleep.

At 6 a.m., Jessica's phone pinged and there was a text message from an unknown phone number.

If you ever want to see the boy again, don't call the cops or FBI. I'll text you further instructions later

Jessica just about broke one of Sam's ribs, elbowing him to wake up, so she could show him the text on her phone.

"Should we call the FBI? Can they trace it?" he asked while rubbing his eyes.

"If we were on the mainland, I would say yes. But in this case we're going to call Gabbie because we need someone we know and can trust to have our backs in this thing. I'm sure the phone's a burner so there's no tracing it."

That morning Jessica called Gabbie and told her someone had abducted Henry and asked her to come back to Kona on the next available flight.

Before Gabbie arrived on the evening flight from Los Angeles, Jessica got another text. This one had a link to a webpage for further instructions. She and Sam opened the link on a desktop computer in the study and what they saw horrified them. It was a video of Henry in a barely lit room. It only showed him sitting on the floor leaning against a wall crying for his Auntie Jessica.

The video then changed from Henry to a man standing next to the boy with a large butcher knife and wearing a black ski-mask. "Jessica Kealoha, you will pay for killing my brother. The price is going to be a life for a life."

The computer screen then had white text that scrolled across the bottom that said, "Wait for further instructions."

After the video was over and the screen went black, Sam asked Jessica what the kidnapper was talking about.

"Vlad Volkov is what he's talking about. That was Ivan's brother. There was a shootout at a motel when I was on the job in LA. It was a him or me situation and I put Vlad down. There was no other choice."

IVAN VOLKOV HAD STALKED Sam and Jessica after he made his way back to Hawaii from Australia, still seeking an opportunity to avenge the death of his brother Vlad.

When he saw Henry with them a couple of times, he did some research online and found the newspaper story talking about Henry being adopted by billionaire Sam Stewart and Jessica Kealoha. That was when he formed the first stage of his plan for revenge, by snatching the boy the first chance he got.

When Ivan Volkov followed them to the birthday party at

Spencer Beach Park he saw it as the perfect time to make his move. When Henry wandered off to the bathroom by himself it was the opportunity Ivan had been waiting for. Ivan had been watching the little boy through binoculars from the parking lot and couldn't believe his luck when he saw the boy all alone.

It only took a minute to lure Henry to Volkov's car with the promise of showing him a puppy, and then snatch him up and drive away.

S am and Jessica picked Gabbie up at the Kona airport that evening and gave her a full report on what had happened so far as they drove towards Kailua town.

When they got to their house at Keauhou Bay they all sat down at the kitchen table and formed a plan how they would deal with Volkov. It was just going to be them. Uncle Jack had left for a fishing trip the week before and was out of cell phone range for the next few days.

The next morning they were all sitting at the breakfast table in the kitchen. And just like Volkov said, Jessica got another text with a link to a webpage. This time there wasn't a video. Just text. And the instructions were clear.

Jessica was to shoot herself in the head with a handgun; Sam was to video it and upload the video to YouTube. After the video was uploaded he was then to text Volkov a link to it. Volkov would then drop Henry off at a public location and text Jessica's phone the location after he viewed the video to confirm Jessica was dead.

Sam shook his head no. "He's insane!"

Jessica nodded in agreement and then Gabbie stunned them when she said, "We're going to do exactly what he said--

sort of." Then she continued, "The Big Island movie people will create the video. The last time I was here, I read in the newspaper all about how they had built a new studio in Kona."

Gabbie made a few phone calls and found out the only guy that had the skills to make a realistic video, like the one they needed, was in Hollywood. He was working on one of the biggest movies of the year. According to his secretary at the Kona studio, he wouldn't be back anytime soon.

Gabbie's face said it all after she got off the phone.

"The guy we need is named Seth Edwards, and he's unavailable because he's doing some big movie in Hollywood right now."

Jessica looked at Sam, "Didn't you paddle with him last season?"

Sam nodded as he pulled out his phone and clicked the home button. "Call Mike," he said.

"Yes, sir," Captain Mike Thompson answered.

"We're going to Burbank. We need to leave in an hour."

"The plane is fueled and ready to go, Mr. Stewart. I'll get to the airport and start the pre-flight. It'll be ready to go when you arrive, sir."

Jessica had been filing her nails during this whole time, too upset to eat. She looked up at Sam and said, "What makes you think he'll just drop what he's doing and make a video for us?"

"His girlfriend and his wife. I'm sure he doesn't want them to ever meet."

"Now that sounds like some yummy shit," Gabbie said, just before taking a sip of coffee.

"One time when we paddled together his wife showed up after the race and Seth was nowhere to be found. I knew he was upstairs in the King Kam hotel swapping spit with his girlfriend and I covered for him. I didn't want to, but it was a bad situation either way. So I elected to keep my mouth shut and let karma be the judge. Besides, his wife was doing the pool boy according to him. He told me the only reason he didn't want a divorce was because of the cost."

"So if he doesn't want to help us...?" Gabbie asked.

Sam smiled. "It's leverage. I'm sure he still doesn't want to give up half of his ten-million-dollar house out at the Four Seasons."

"You mean blackmail," Jessica countered.

"I like leverage better," Gabbie said.

Sam smiled. "I'm sure he'll be happy to take a day out of his busy schedule and help us out."

Gabbie stayed behind, Sam and Jessica went to the airport. Captain Mike was sitting in the cockpit ready to go when Sam and Jessica boarded the aircraft. As soon as the door was closed the Captain spun up the engines and taxied to the runway. The Gulfstream jet climbed out of Kona towards the US mainland. While they were en route over the Pacific Jessica used the satellite phone on the plane to call her old partner Sal Romano at Hollywood Robbery-Homicide Division.

She gave him a rundown of what had happened and asked him if he could help locate Seth Edwards who was in Burbank. She had found Seth's studio phone number online, and tried to call him, but the receptionist stonewalled her no matter what Jessica said. Sal said, "No problem. Call me when you land."

It was a smooth flight and landed in Burbank five hours later at about four in the afternoon.

Sal had worked Robbery-Homicide Division for years and knew how to find people who didn't want to be found. Since Seth Edwards wasn't trying to hide, Sal had him located in under an hour.

Sal was waiting on the ramp with airport police when the Gulfstream jet taxied to a stop.

When the door of the plane opened, the wind was blowing, the smell of jet fuel permeating the air as Sam and Jessica came off the plane. Sal was standing at the bottom of the staircase. Jessica yelled, "This is Sam." He and Sal shook hands as they rushed to a waiting unmarked police SUV. Jessica didn't expect the police escort to the studio, but she was grateful for all the extra attention Sal had shown her and Sam that day.

As they were leaving the airport, Sal said, "I took a drive over to his studio earlier. I knew right where it was, there's a great little Italian place around the corner from it that I eat at all the time. He's expecting us, I gave him what you told me. And told him I was picking you up at the airport and I would bring you back to the studio to see him. You think this movie guy can help you?" Sal asked, as they sped over to the studio.

Jessica sat there in the front seat of the Ford SUV as they blew through red lights with lights flashing and the siren wailing. She was holding a pressure point on her hand, just above the thumb, trying to get rid of a tension headache when she answered Sal. "I don't know, it's the only play we have right now."

Sam interjected from the backseat, "The kidnapper gave us twenty-four hours to produce the video or else he would kill our son Henry—and still continue to come after Jessica."

❦

THEY ARRIVED at the movie studio office of Seth Edwards and were greeted by a young woman with bleach blond hair wearing a mini-skirt and a tube top. Before she had a chance to say anything Sal pulled out his badge and showed it to her.

"We're here to see Mr. Edwards. He's expecting us." Jessica said, while the woman stared at Sal's badge.

The young woman pranced in six-inch stiletto heels to a door off to the side of the room and motioned the trio to follow her.

Everyone thought making a fake snuff film was worth a

try. Except Seth Edwards.

"I can't make this video you need in fifteen minutes. And surely not by the morning deadline even if we got to work right now. I'm sorry, there's just not enough time."

Seth frowned and then looked at Sam and said, "I know I owe you and I would drop what I'm doing to help, but there just isn't enough time. Again, I'm very sorry."

⁊

SAM AND JESSICA left the studio devastated. They thanked Sal for all of his help, that was for naught, and flew back to Kona that night.

7 a.m. the next morning they were sitting at the breakfast table just like the day before. But now they had no plan and no time left before the deadline to have a snuff film uploaded for Ivan Volkov to see. The only thing different was Gabbie wasn't there. But she had texted Jessica. She was working on something and would let them know by 8:30 a.m. if it was going to pan out.

Sam and Jessica sat across the table from each other, staring at the bay and not saying a word. They were both too upset to eat breakfast and then Jessica said softly, "We have to do it."

Sam's face wrinkled up as if his nose was recoiling from the smell of death.

"No, just no, don't even talk like that," he said in a firm tone of voice.

"It's because of me Aimee is dead and Henry doesn't have a mother..." Sam interrupted and raised his voice. "If you're dead he still won't have a mother. So just erase any more thoughts coming into your head of going through with Volkov's demand."

Jessica had been suffering from PTSD for some time, and had thought about killing herself more than once and probably would have, if she had not quit drinking. But this time it had nothing to do with wanting to commit suicide. Without realizing it, she had truly become Henry's mother when she was willing to trade her life for his.

She and Sam got into a heated discussion about what the next step should be when Gabbie walked through the front door.

"Good news." That stopped Sam and Jessica in mid-sentence before things that could never be taken back were said.

"So what is this good news?" They both asked in unison as if they were operating on one brain.

"I called in some favors and I've got Special Agents from the Florida FBI office working on this. It turns out Volkov has pissed off the Russian mob in Florida too. He's a dead man if they ever find him. Somehow he figured out a way to hack one of their offshore accounts and drained all the cash out of it. Word on the street is there's a contract out on him now."

"I'll double it," Sam said. Both Gabbie and Jessica cut their eyes toward Sam with a look of disapproval.

"The video you will upload this morning is one where you tell him he has one chance to save his own life, and this is it."

After Gabbie went over the details of what they should say, that's exactly what Sam and Jessica did twenty minutes later.

They sat together on the couch in the living room, and Jessica did the talking as Gabbie shot the video. Sam had his arm around her as she sat there calm and unemotional; her Japanese side was at its best.

"I shot your brother Vlad because he left me no choice." There was a tinge of annoyance in her voice.

"If you're too stupid to understand that."

"Cut" Gabbie said.

"Let's try it again minus the stupid part."

Jessica nodded, and they started over.

"Your brother gave me no choice. I'm sorry it had to happen. But here's the thing Ivan, if you hurt Henry you're going to die a slow painful death."

Jessica stopped for a second to take a sip of water and then she continued.

"If you do not release Henry, we will put a bounty on your head of one million dollars. And we will raise the bounty until you are found and disposed of one little piece at a time. Right now we are chartering planes in Florida and Australia to bring every known Russian mobster you have ripped off to Hawaii. We may not find you, but they will."

Jessica paused again.

"You have one hour to drop Henry off at any of the big box stores in Kona, with a note in his pocket to give them with my phone number. In return, you get to continue living."

Jessica turned toward Sam. It was his turn to talk into the camera.

"Think about this, we love Henry, and if you hurt him, we will see to it that you die a horrible death. There won't be anywhere on this planet you will be able to hide."

Gabbie stopped the recording.

"That's good."

Sam turned to Jessica.

"When this is over you're going to see someone. Psychiatrist or psychologist, I don't care, it's your choice, but you will go see someone."

She reluctantly nodded in agreement. Volunteering to off herself to save Henry was a sure sign going to see a shrink might not be a bad idea. If nothing else, to work out that this time it wasn't about harming herself for any reason other than wanting to save Henry's life.

Now they would wait to see what Volkov would do. In the meantime, Sam and Jessica would pay Larry Black a visit to find out what he knew about Volkov.

20

I van watched the video reply from Sam and Jessica. It didn't surprise him they didn't go through with it. But he didn't quite expect the scorched earth response he got from them either.

In the beginning it was all about revenge until he learned that Sam Stewart was a billionaire and he thought about it for a while. Jessica's death would have helped Ivan feel some sense of justice. But in his mind there was nothing like millions of dollars in cold cash to ease the pain of the loss of his brother Vlad. Now it was going to be all about the money.

Ivan thought if they're willing to pay a million dollars for people to kill him, maybe they would be willing to pay five million to have Henry back instead. It was worth a try, he thought.

But first, there was only one thing to do in a situation like this. Have a drink and think about how to implement his new plan.

Ivan's drink of choice was like a lot of Russians, vodka. But the thing was, sometimes he planned to only have one drink and after having that drink he would go on a binge.

The next day he would wake up wondering what the hell happened the night before.

The TV was on and Henry was sitting on the floor watching it. He wasn't crying anymore because Ivan had convinced him Sam and Jessica wanted Ivan to watch him for a few days until they could pick him up.

Ivan's brain was in a fog as he looked around the room. Henry continued to watch TV while munching on a spam musabi.

"Where did you get that?" Ivan asked him.

"The lady gave it to me last night." Henry turned back around and took another bite of his rice and spam with his eyes glued to the TV.

Ivan had no idea what the young boy was talking about. But later that morning he noticed his wallet was short five hundred dollars and surmised he must have called a hooker while he was in a drunken blackout.

Ivan made another video and texted Jessica. In this video he thought he'd take a different approach and showed Henry sitting on the floor watching cartoons. He ignored the fact she hadn't killed herself as he had demanded before. He also ignored the video where Sam and Jessica said he was dead if he didn't return Henry.

"Maybe my original demand was a little extreme," he said in broken English.

"I have a new proposition for you. Five million dollars and you can have the boy back. This offer is only good for twenty-four hours. Then the price goes to ten million. And after that? I take him on a one-way fishing trip and use him for bait. I will text you the account number of an offshore account to wire the money to later today. If you do not transfer the money within fifteen minutes of my text, there'll be no second text ever again and the boy will be dead."

21

Afterr Sam and Jessica had made the video telling Volkov he was a dead man if he didn't return Henry, they went to see Larry Black. And Gabbie paid a visit to the Kona PD. Gabbie wanted to see about getting them to look harder for Volkov and Henry.

Sam and Jessica both thought Larry might be able to help find Ivan Volkov and Henry. Sam had suspected for a long time that Larry was laundering money for the Russian mob. After they took Volkov at gunpoint from HSI agents, Uncle Jack said that Homeland Security agreed with Jessica's hypothesis that they smuggled Volkov out of the country aboard the *Akula* since it left Kailua Bay on the same day they hijacked him from HSI.

Uncle Jack also told Sam and Jessica that Larry Black might not have been fishing, but he sure as hell stunk like a fish when it came to being involved with Volkov's escape.

Besides building super yachts for the ultra-rich, Sam invested in a lot of real estate on the island. He saw too many deals run through Larry's brokerage that made no sense financially. Larry's clients always paid over market value. Laundering money was the only thing that made sense.

Sam valued Larry's business of bringing ultra-wealthy yacht buyers to his boat building company and wanted to be diplomatic but firm. Jessica, on the other hand, wanted to stick a gun in Larry's face to get some answers.

Sam called Larry and told him that he and Jessica needed to see him, and that it was an emergency.

Larry was pressed for time but agreed to a quick meeting at the Kona Inn Restaurant. It was within walking distance of another meeting he had scheduled that afternoon.

&.

SAM AND JESSICA were seated at a table on the outdoor patio at Kona Inn waiting for Larry, who was running a few minutes behind. With a view of Kailua Bay, Jessica was watching a tour boat come in from an early morning snorkel tour at Kealakekua Bay. Sam was looking at his phone checking his email while they waited. The pier was a beehive of activity that day as boats came and went.

The waitress had brought ice teas to the table and sat them down, turned and walked away. Jessica, who was already annoyed, stared at the lemon wedge in her tea like a cat watching a bug; it just about put her over the edge.

"Yuck," she said, as she pulled the slice from her glass. She was a self-admitted germaphobe and there were certain things that had to be right in her world. And lemon wedges in restaurant tea was high on her list of things that grossed her out.

Minutes later after Larry arrived and sat down at the table, he gave the waitress his drink order. Jessica scooted closer to the table and leaned toward Larry and said, "We've been in contact with Volkov, he's holding our son Henry for ransom."

Larry didn't say anything but called the waitress back to the table and changed his order from iced tea to vodka.

Jessica's eyes bore into Larry's. She continued, "You're going to need that drink. I don't doubt for a second you know who abducted Volkov from HSI at the airport. As far as I'm concerned, you're involved with them somehow." Sam nodded in agreement.

She continued, "If your buddies hadn't abducted Volkov, he wouldn't have escaped and come back here and kidnapped our son." Jessica leaned back in her chair and glared at Larry as she mashed her teeth together.

Sam reached over and rubbed her shoulder as she continued to stare Larry in the eye.

The waitress dropped off Larry's drink and then went off to deliver other orders to tables nearby. Larry picked up the shot glass of vodka and downed it.

It was Sam's turn, "Volkov wants us to pay a ransom, we're not doing that. Instead, we're putting a bounty on his head."

Larry nodded and then said, "I have a lot of contacts that I can reach out to. I'll see what I can do to help you get your son back."

Jessica leaned forward toward Larry and said, "We appreciate that Larry, because the last thing you want is the Feds knee deep in your business. Because if anything happens to Henry I promise you'll swing with Volkov. It's not a threat. It's a promise."

Larry nodded he understood and threw a twenty-dollar bill down on the table and then got up and left without saying a word.

22

After Larry Black left the meeting with Sam and Jessica, he drove back to his office at the harbor. He muttered to himself the entire way about how he should have never gotten involved in the whole affair with Ivan Volkov.

Larry and Sam had done a lot of business together in the past year, and Sam had told him in casual conversation over a few beers that Jessica was a former homicide detective. Sam had even bragged that she had broken a lot of big cases in LA over her twenty-one-year career.

There was no doubt in Larry's mind she could make serious trouble for him if she wanted to.

He needed to make a phone call to his silent business partner, and he only used a burner phone that he kept in his office safe to contact her.

"Your people made a mess. Volkov has kidnapped Jessica Kealoha's kid. She's threatening to call the Feds to investigate my business if I don't help her and Sam Stewart get their kid back. And if the Feds look at me, you're eventually going to be on their radar, too."

"So that's where he went." The woman on the other end of the line paused for a moment and then said in a calm matter-of-fact tone of voice, "Don't worry, I'll take care of Jessica Kealoha."

"How, like your people took care of Volkov?" Larry said, with a sharp tone of voice.

"I'll have my best people eliminate the threat."

"Whoa, whoa, whoa. You can't do that. She's a former cop and the wife of Sam Stewart, the CEO of Stewart Industries. There will be serious repercussions. That guy has connections at the highest levels of government and he will bring us nothing but pain. If you want to bump off someone like Volkov, fine, but Jessica Kealoha is a bad idea."

"Don't you think I have as much or more influence? I don't care who her husband is, we can weather the storm and then it will be back to business as usual. And remember this, I tell you, you don't tell me."

Before Larry could say another word, she hung up the phone.

He slumped back into his chair disgusted and threw the burner phone in the garbage can next to his desk.

He didn't mind white-collar crime like money laundering. But murder? Not anymore. In the old country it was part of doing business. But that was a line he had no interest crossing anymore.

He felt he had no choice but to warn Jessica that her life was once again in danger. This time by a Russian oligarch named Alina Evanoff. And unlike Volkov, Evanoff would send professional killers to handle the job, or she might even do it herself given the right circumstances.

If she ever found out Larry tipped off Jessica, he was as good as dead too. If he didn't kill her first.

23

Gabbie Harris had been busy while Sam and Jessica had their meeting with Larry Black at the Kona Inn. She had bugged his office and car while he was with them. Earlier that day Jessica told Gabbie where Larry's office was and that his car was a silver Bentley. She also told Gabbie there was about a ninety-nine percent chance she would find it in the parking lot behind Uncle Billy's Motel at around noon. Sam had told Jessica, Larry was there every Wednesday afternoon. At the time when he had told her that, Jessica lifted an eyebrow and said, "Your car had better not ever be 'known' to be parked at the no tell motel on a certain day every week."

Sam and Jessica had returned home and were waiting for the text from Volkov. Even though they had told Volkov and Larry Black they would pay the Russian mob to hunt him down, privately they had agreed that they would pay the ransom to get Henry back. And the bounty on Volkov's head would still stand.

Sam was ready to transfer the five million into Volkov's account if and when the text came in.

Jessica's phone rang a few minutes after they got home. It was lying on the coffee table and both she and Sam rushed to see who the call was from. Sam flew back into the couch disappointed almost as fast as he leaned forward when he saw it was from Gabbie.

Jessica picked up the phone and clicked the speaker button and sat it back down on the table so Sam could hear the conversation, too. Then she asked Gabbie, "Did you get it done?"

"I got it done, both the office and the car. I barely got out of his office before he came back. But here's the thing, Larry Black made a call, but it wasn't from the office phone. He must have used his cell phone or a burner. I wouldn't think he's dumb enough to use his cell for the type of call that he made. I could only hear his part of the conversation because I put two bugs in there, one in the office phone and one under his desk."

"So what did he say?" Jessica asked.

"He told whoever he was talking to that you would sic the Feds on him if he didn't help you get Henry back." Gabbie paused for just a moment and then continued, "Near as I could tell, from his reaction, someone on the other end of the line said they were going to put out a contract on you."

There was silence on the line for a second before Jessica told Gabbie to come back to the house so they could get a plan together, after they had dealt with getting Henry back first.

❦

THIS TIME when there was a knock at the front door, when it opened, it was Jessica standing there with a 9mm Glock in her hand. She tucked it back into her waistband holster behind her back, and held the door open for Gabbie to come into the house.

Sam was talking on his phone, while sitting at the dining room table, when Gabbie and Jessica entered the room.

"I've got security on the way. But it will be light because I rarely need many people in Kona."

"What does light mean?" Gabbie asked.

"Ten guys. I'll have them stay in the guest house and try to stay out of sight as much as possible."

This time Jessica would not argue. She would take all the help she could get, even if it meant they had to stay inside the main house. She didn't have time for this, all she wanted to focus on right now was getting Henry back.

Jessica was used to people saying they would kill her but Sam, not so much. The thing that stuck in the back of her mind was the men that took Volkov at gunpoint at the airport. They were not your run-of-the-mill thugs. No, these guys were pros, and she had to respect them for the danger they posed. For the first time since retiring from the LAPD, Jessica thought about going back into law enforcement. It was the only way she could ever carry a gun legally on the island. But working for the Kona PD was a non-starter for her.

24

Twenty-four hours had passed, and Sam and Jessica had still not received a text from Volkov with instructions on where to wire the ransom money. And true to their word, there were two planes coming from Florida and Australia with Russian mobsters to hunt him down. Unknown to Sam and Jessica, some of them were on the payroll of Alina Evanoff and their mission wasn't to find Henry but to carry out the contract on Jessica.

Sam and Jessica sat at the table in the kitchen cleaning their guns, and didn't say over two words to each other, while the ominous soundtrack to the House of Cards TV show played in the background. Even though Henry had been in their life only a short time, they loved him as their own. Not knowing where he was and if he was okay was almost more than they could bear.

Jessica finished putting her Glock back together, jumped up from the table and grabbed her purse. "I can't sit here and wait anymore. I have to go look for him."

"Where are you going?" Sam asked.

"I don't know, I just know I can't sit here anymore."

Jessica was heading for the door when Sam stopped her with a single sentence.

"You want to get married?"

She turned and looked at him for a moment before answering.

"After we get Henry back." And then she walked out the front door with her Glock tucked into the waistband of her Levi's. She wore a baggy light blue, long sleeve shirt of Sam's to cover it.

Sam yelled, "Wait for me!" He hurried to finish putting his gun back together.

* * *

GABBIE WAS out in front of the house talking to Sam's security team, when she saw Jessica heading for her Toyota 4Runner parked in the driveway.

"Where do you think you're going?" she barked as she met Jessica at the door of the truck.

"To look for Henry."

"Oh, no you're not! Back in the house, lady. Remember those hired killers coming here to kill your ass?"

Sam stood there and watched from the front door of the house as Gabbie told Jessica how it would be, in a way that he would never have been able to.

"I can't stay here and do nothing Gabbie."

"I know honey, we'll find Henry, but you got to sit tight for now. It's the right thing to do."

Jessica knew Gabbie was right; she turned around and walked back into the house. The last thing she needed was to get pulled over and arrested for carrying a concealed firearm. And getting a concealed carry permit on the Big Island would never happen, since the chief of police staunchly opposed civilians carrying guns. In a newspaper interview the chief said he wouldn't issue a concealed carry permit under any circumstance.

Sam, Jessica, and Gabbie went into the house to talk about what the next step would be. Jessica's phone pinged as she sat down on the couch that faced the bay view windows over-looking Keauhou Bay.

It was Uncle Jack. He had stopped off in Honolulu, on his way back to the Big Island, from his fishing trip near Midway Island. He was back on the island and had news from a meeting with the governor of Hawaii. The text read:

The gov said he has directed the Hawaii County Sheriff's Department to put a task force together, and he wants you on it because of your experience with serial killers, we'll talk later

Sam and Gabbie were standing behind the couch, leaning over Jessica's shoulder, reading her text thinking it might be from Volkov.

"That's the last thing I need right now," Jessica groaned.

"Au contraire, that's exactly what you need after this situation with Henry is over," Gabbie shot back.

25

The Gulfstream jet from Florida touched down on the Kona runway at eight thirty-seven in the morning. There were six Russian mobsters aboard. All of them had extensive criminal histories. A couple of them were suspects in the murders of known rivals in the Russian criminal underworld in Florida.

Gabbie was at the airport waiting with a shuttle to take them to Aloha Village, where Jessica had set aside a couple of bungalows for them to stay in. The village was perfectly situated on the Kona coast in terms of location to all the other resort areas. Jessica suspected Ivan Volkov would be hiding out at one of the resorts and told Gabbie to relay that information to the Russians.

To ease any fears about the million-dollar bounty, Gabbie brought armed security with her, and a duffle bag containing a million dollars in cash. The money was in a secondary SUV to show the Russians that all they had to do was find Volkov, bring Henry back and the money was theirs.

Gabbie met the six rough looking men at the bottom of the jet's staircase. That morning the balmy breeze blew through her hair as she waited for the door of the plane to open. The air smelled of jet fuel. The sounds of a busy airport filled the air with inter-island jets coming and going, and the helicopter school choppers taking off and landing nearby.

The six mercenaries came off the plane and Gabbie marched them over to a nearby Chevy Tahoe. She opened the rear door to show them she had a million dollars, in cash in an unzipped duffle bag, and was prepared to pay for the return of Henry. As far as Sam and Jessica were concerned, the Russians could do whatever they wanted with Volkov.

One of the men was wearing a short-sleeve shirt and his arms were covered in Russian gang tattoos. He was the leader of the group and named Alexei Dmitrievich. He looked Gabbie in the eye and said in broken English, "What's stopping us from taking the money, getting back on the plane and leaving? You don't think you will stop us, do you?"

Gabbie shook her head no.

"But they will."

She turned her head to the left. There was a helicopter hovering a hundred feet off the deck nearby. "Notice the sniper with a rifle pointed at you." Dmitrievich looked toward the chopper. Gabbie turned her head back toward him, and jutted her chin, to motion him to look behind him. Dmitrievich turned around and looked toward the top of the jet's staircase; he saw the pilot and copilot holding AR-15's.

The old Russian turned back, smiled at Gabbie and said, "You've made your point. Besides, we want Volkov and would have hunted him for free, since your people were kind enough to narrow down his location for us. The money is just a bonus. But we'll take it."

The six Russians piled into the shuttle van waiting to take them to Aloha Village.

Gabbie had her poker face on while staring at the weathered face of evil. Just the sight of Alexei Dmitrievich sent a chill down her spine. If she had to dance with the devil to help Jessica get Henry back, then that is exactly what she would do. If her boss at FBI headquarters ever got wind of what she was involved in, she would most likely lose her job. She might even be prosecuted for operating outside the boundaries of the law. But she owed Jessica and now it was time to pay it back. Even if she lost her job over it. Or faced going to jail.

26

Two Days Later

The Russians had quickly narrowed down which hotel Ivan was staying at, by calling every resort on the island. They told the clerks they were looking for a dangerous Russian who had escaped from a mental institution overseas.

When making those calls, they also told them they would pay a thousand dollars for each name and room number of every Russian staying in their hotel. That amount of money quashed any confidentiality obligation the clerks may have felt toward guests in the hotel.

In less than twenty-four hours of being on the island, Alexei Dmitrievich had a list of five Russians staying on the west side of the island. The mobsters went to each hotel and checked every lead looking for Ivan Volkov. The last hotel on the list was the King Kam in the village.

When Alexei Dmitrievich called the King Kam, the clerk said they didn't have anyone with a Russian passport staying there. But they did have a guy who checked in recently using a German passport. The clerk remembered him because he thought it was odd the man had a Russian accent and a German passport.

Alexei Dmitrievich brought all of his men to look for Ivan at the King Kam. It was the last hotel to check, and he could feel it in his bones that this was where Ivan Volkov was hiding.

꙳

IVAN VOLKOV WAS nothing like his brother, Vlad. His older brother would have killed Henry a long time ago as revenge and never thought twice about it.

Ivan was much younger than Vlad and wasn't a vicious killer. He was more of an opportunistic type of criminal, into committing crimes that didn't require being face-to-face. Which was why he chose to be a hacker.

For Ivan, trying to kill Jessica was about revenge for his older brother's death. Even if Sam and Jessica did not pay the ransom, Ivan wouldn't kill Henry. He didn't have the stomach for it.

The funny thing was, he started playing video games with Henry on the TV in the hotel room; he even enjoyed playing with the little guy—a lot. Henry was not like your typical five-year-old. He was used to being passed off to different people, when he was with his mother, and quickly adapted to his surroundings. Before she got sober, she would leave him with various people on a regular basis when she went off on a bender.

Ivan started thinking about Henry almost like he was a little brother. The thought occurred to him he should just forget about the ransom. He could take Henry, leave the island as soon as possible and go back to Europe. They could live in Prague, play video games, and he could hack a bank every once in a while to pay the bills. It would be great.

Ivan Volkoff had decided he would take Henry with him to Prague. He had the airline tickets lined up and everything was ready to go. All he needed to do was go downstairs to the ABC store and pick up some snacks for the long trip.

A few minutes later Ivan was standing in the aisle of the ABC store inside the hotel. He was looking at all the Japanese snacks, like wasabi nuts, noting that he'd never make the same mistake twice of putting a handful of them in his mouth.

When he glanced down the aisle to his right toward the back of the store where the coolers were, he saw a man that had his back to him. He thought nothing about it until the man opened the cooler to grab a drink. That's when Ivan saw the Russian gang tattoo on top of the man's right hand as he reached in the cooler. Ivan immediately bolted from the store, going back upstairs to his room using the fire escape stairwell, being as stealthy as possible. He knew this time he was a dead man if the Russian mob found him—there would be no talking his way out of it.

Ivan had a room in the hotel overlooking Palani Road. He immediately pulled the curtains closed to prevent anyone from looking in from the Seaside Hotel across the street.

Ivan knew most of those guys in the mob were ex-KGB; they were relentless. They would find him eventually if he didn't get off the island that day.

He packed his carry-on bag as fast as he could. His plan, before the Russians showed up, would be to take an Uber to the airport. But now he had to make it to a location somewhere away from the hotel to catch a ride. There was no way he and Henry could stand in front of the hotel for ten or fifteen minutes waiting for an Uber, without the Russians seeing him and the boy.

Volkov decided his best chance to escape was to take Henry, walk down the fire escape and out a side entrance of the hotel, thus avoiding the lobby and elevators because they would be under surveillance by Dmitrievich's men.

27

E very week Larry Black rendezvoused with a hooker at the King Kam hotel. Her nickname was Anto, short for Antonina. Antonina Svetlana was a thirty-two-year-old former real estate agent at Larry's firm.

She tried selling real estate for a few years during the downturn in the market but didn't have the stomach for the dog-eat-dog world of it. At the time Larry had tried everything to get her in bed, and hinted more than once, he was willing to pay for it. He phrased it as more like an arrangement.

Anto was a tall blonde, who was hit on daily, so she thought she might as well sell her services instead of giving it away. After making six figures the first year turning tricks, in a down economy, she was never going back to real estate. Besides, she knew her clients' goal was to screw her and pay five hundred dollars an hour for it; she was okay with that. Unlike real estate, where sometimes she got screwed and not paid.

If there ever was a guy in love with a hooker, it was Larry Black. It was seven thirty in the morning after he had his morning swim at the pier. He called Anto to reschedule their weekly date. After he missed his last appointment with her, because of the meeting with Sam and Jessica, he was eager to make up his time.

"Sure, honey, let's meet up at the King Kam in an hour," she purred and then hung up the phone.

An hour later Larry walked into the lobby of the hotel and glanced at a guy who appeared to be reading a newspaper. Except he wasn't. It was Alexei Dmitrievich. Once again it was a tattoo that tipped off Larry.

The hair on the back of his neck stood up. Larry recognized him from a photo Alina Evanoff had shown of him before. Alina Evanoff and Alexei Dmitrievich were sworn enemies.

At one time she had talked of taking over the Florida mob and wanted Larry to move to Florida to help facilitate the coup. Larry told her no way, since he knew there was an excellent chance of him getting murdered in the deal.

Larry had no idea Sam and Jessica had flown in the mob from Florida. He needed to call Alina and let her know what was going on, but this time he wasn't going to miss his appointment with Anto.

❧

LARRY AND ANTO were lying in bed. She was on her side with her head propped up on a pillow, rubbing circles in Larry's chest hair with her right hand, while he lay on his back staring at the ceiling.

"What's wrong, baby? You seem tense today," she said.

Larry never had a problem getting it up before. He had a lot on his mind, and this was the icing on the cake for the week he was having.

Larry let out a big sigh and then started to talk.

"Some guy kidnaps a kid from an associate of mine and a long story short. If I don't help find this kid I'm in deep kimchi. A Russian named Ivan Volkov scooped him up and wants a big ransom from my business associate or he will off this kid."

Anto abruptly stopped rubbing Larry's chest and asked, "Is this kid about four or five years old and have shiny black hair?"

Larry sat straight up as if a hot poker had prodded him in the middle of his back.

"You've seen this kid?"

"I think so. Two or three nights ago I had a date here in the hotel. The guy had a young boy fitting that description in his room asleep. The kid woke up in the middle of it and I gave him something to eat while we finished up."

"Do you remember what room he was in?"

"No, I was super high that night and am lucky to remember it even happened. I am pretty sure it was on the third floor, somewhere in the middle of the hallway, on the mauka side of the building."

Larry grabbed his phone off the nightstand and clicked the button to speed dial Sam.

When Sam answered the phone he waved at Jessica, who was in the kitchen making coffee, to come over and listen to what Larry Black had to say.

"Hey Larry, what's up?"

"Henry is what's up. I will give you the tip you've been waiting for, but you got to promise me this gets Jessica to back off from calling the Feds about my business."

Sam looked at Jessica and she nodded it was a deal.

"Consider it a deal," Sam said.

After Larry told them what Anto had said, Jessica grabbed her Glock and headed for the door, with Sam and Gabbie in hot pursuit. There was no stopping her this time.

28

Alexei Dmitrievich and his crew from Florida had the King Kam surrounded, as well as six guys could ever hope to. They had been to the room the hotel clerk said Volkov was staying in many times. Nobody answered the door and there was no sound coming from the room.

The hotel clerk was willing to give Dmitrievich the room number, but that was as far as it would go, since Dmitrievich said they were bounty hunters and not cops. Which was obvious even to a casual observer given some of their tattoos.

Alexei Dmitrievich brought a spy cam with him for such an event and stuck it under the door to verify the room was empty. After he was sure the room was vacant, he waited down in the lobby to see if Volkov would come back to the room, since the clerk said Volkov had paid for the entire week.

❧

SAM, Jessica, and Gabbie arrived at the hotel twenty minutes after Larry had called. When they entered the hotel lobby

Gabbie zeroed in on Alexei Dmitrievich sitting there pretending to be reading a newspaper. She whispered to Sam and Jessica who he was as they walked by. When Sam and Jessica got to the elevator, Gabbie doubled back to see what he was up to. While she went to talk to him, Sam and Jessica went straight to the third floor and started knocking on doors.

About twenty percent of the people staying at the hotel on that floor opened their doors. None of them had seen Henry except for one guy. He said he saw a little boy, who fit the description, and a man get in the elevator earlier that morning. When Jessica showed the man a picture of Henry, he said that was him for sure.

The man also mentioned a rather scary looking fellow with a European accent had knocked on his door earlier that morning, asking about the same kid. He told the man he hadn't seen the boy. At the time that was true, because it wasn't until later that morning he saw Henry and Volkov get in the elevator.

Sam and Jessica went down to the lobby, and motioned to Gabbie to come with them, as they headed out the door to their Chevy Tahoe parked at the curb.

As the Tahoe left the hotel parking lot, Jessica filled Gabbie in and asked what Dmitrievich had to say.

"He thinks Volkov will come back to the hotel. I told him we had a lead we were checking out there and he interrupted me. He said he already knows Volkov is staying at the King Kam and he will stay there and wait for him to return. And don't even think about screwing him out of the reward money."

❦

IVAN AND HENRY had slipped out of the hotel unnoticed that

morning and caught a taxi to the Waimea airport where security would be almost non-existent. From there they would take an island hopper to Maui, where they would board a flight to the US mainland, and then continue on to Prague.

29

The Tahoe pulled into the driveway at their home in Keauhou and Sam parked right outside the front door in case they needed to leave in a hurry again.

"If you don't mind I'd like to use your computer in the study," Gabbie asked.

"Sure, go ahead," Sam answered.

Sam and Jessica knew that the contract put out on her life came from an associate of Larry Black, thanks to Gabbie bugging his office.

They also knew there was a good chance one or more of the Russians, on the second plane coming from Australia, was hired to make the hit.

Sam called the pilot of the second Gulfstream jet he had chartered in Gold Coast, Australia and told him to abort the flight to Hawaii and return to Gold Coast.

"Roger that, Mr. Stewart," was the reply and as far as Sam knew he had resolved that problem for the time being.

❦

SITTING at Sam's desk in the study, Gabbie had gone back

through the recording from the bug she put in Larry's Bentley. She had caught something she missed the first time she had listened to the recording. It was a name mentioned when Larry was ranting to himself about getting involved with locating Volkov. It was hard to hear because a car pulled up next to Larry at what must have been a stop light. The other car had its stereo blasting making it impossible to hear what Larry was saying. It wasn't until the light turned green, and Larry sped away from the mobile ghetto blaster, that the recording became clear again.

Gabbie still couldn't understand what the name was after listening to the recording over and over. She finally gave up and emailed the audio file to the FBI lab in Quantico, Virginia to see if they could clean up the audio and decipher what the name was.

It was an easy one for the tech working that day at the FBI crime lab. He separated the audio from the music tracks and in less than fifteen minutes it was clear the name Larry mentioned on the recording was Alina. He could be heard muttering her name over and over when the boom box was blasting in the car beside him.

With a little research of the Russian mob, it didn't take Gabbie long to figure out Larry was talking about Alina Evanoff. And with a little more digging she found out Ms. Evanoff was the suspected kingpin of the Russian mob in Australia.

Jessica was in the kitchen making a pot of coffee when Gabbie startled her with her findings.

Gabbie said, "Alina Evanoff is who put the contract out on you." And then handed her the photo of the woman.

"Geez Gabbie, you're like a ghost. You need a bell around your neck or something."

Jessica looked at the photo and paused for a second and then said, "She doesn't look familiar and I don't recognize the name either. Who is she?"

"She's the head of the Australian Russian mafia. There's not much known about her other than rumors she was a former KGB agent turned mobster. Apparently, she has murdered her way to the top according to a source I checked with."

Jessica sighed and said, "It must be kill Jessica week in Australia."

"I will say, when you make enemies you do a good job of it."

30

B ecky Kahale showed up for her shift, at Mokulele Air at the Waimea airport, thinking it would be another boring day at the little airport just outside of town.

She walked by where Ivan Volkov and Henry sat in the small terminal waiting for the next flight to Maui. Becky made her way to the gate to start her shift announcing arrivals and departures and collecting boarding passes. She was a one-woman band; it was such a small airport, there was no TSA inspection required, people just showed up with a ticket and boarded the plane.

There was something familiar about the dark-haired little boy sitting there quietly playing with a bug on the floor. Becky continued to do her work and for about a half an hour she kept wondering where she knew that kid from. Maybe it was daycare where she dropped off her own kids. The thought left her mind as she got busy with paperwork before the next flight left.

That day the flight from Maui was late and Ivan Volkov was getting nervous; he asked Becky twice when the plane would arrive. She told him sometimes it was a little late, but it always showed up if that was any consolation.

As Ivan turned and walked back to where he and Henry sat she realized, *that's where I've seen that kid, the Amber Alert.* She didn't recognize Volkov from the televised news coverage because they were showing an older photo of him. He had since changed his appearance by growing a beard and shaving his head.

As Becky ducked down behind the ticket counter to call 911, the flight from Maui landed and would be at the gate in a few minutes.

"I swear it's the kid plastered all over the TV news," she whispered to the 911 operator. "Please hurry, they're getting ready to board a flight to Maui in a few minutes."

The Maui flight was a quick turnaround with just enough time for the flight crew to use the bathroom between legs. Sometimes the pilot and copilot just stayed in the cockpit.

Before Becky collected the boarding passes from each passenger, she jogged out on the ramp to the plane. She needed to talk to the pilot since it looked like he wasn't getting off the plane that day. After she explained the situation, he agreed to keep the plane on the ground until the police arrived. To keep Volkov from becoming suspicious they would board everyone and then the cops could take Henry and Volkov off the plane.

SAM, Jessica and Gabbie were still at the house at Keauhou Bay, and had been listening to the police scanner that day. It was always on since Henry's abduction. As soon as it came over the radio that there was a report of a child, fitting Henry's description for the Amber Alert, the police dispatched an officer to investigate. Jessica started to grab her purse when Gabbie said, "Let's just sit tight until we get confirmation."

Jessica slumped herself down on the couch in the living

room and started to pray. She was still on the fence whether or not there was a god but figured it didn't hurt to act as if there was for the time being.

She couldn't sit still any longer, and called the watch commander over in Waimea to get the latest update whether or not it was Henry.

"Are you kidding me?" Jessica said, in disgust five minutes later.

Sam had been in the shower; he'd just gotten out and walked into the living room. While drying his hair with a towel, he noticed Gabbie and Jessica were in a serious discussion about what they should do.

"What's going on?" he asked.

"Henry's been found, but it's turned into a total disaster over at the airport in Waimea," Jessica answered.

Jessica got up, shoved her Glock in her purse, and looked at Sam. "Let's go," she commanded.

Gabbie didn't bother to argue, since it looked like it would be up to them to free Henry.

After the close call with Jessica having to be flown to the hospital on Maui, Sam wasn't taking any more chances. He had bought a new helicopter, and hired a former Army Apache pilot, named Bob Ford, to fly it.

Sam called Bob, who was at the hanger doing some cleaning and polishing on the new bird. It was a new Eurocopter, touted as the world's fastest civilian chopper and capable of making the thirty-mile trip, to Waimea from the Kona airport, in about ten minutes.

The trio piled in the black armored Tahoe that was still on loan from Uncle Jack.

"I guess if we're going to continue to have so much excitement in our lives maybe I should buy one of these," Sam said, as they were driving to the Kona airport. Neither Gabbie nor Jessica were in the mood for humor that day.

"I wonder if the Russians have a scanner too?" he continued.

Sam was driving and Jessica sat next to him. She turned and looked at him. "Make this thing go faster," she said.

When they arrived at the airport Bob had the chopper out on the ramp and had spun up the engines and was ready to go. Everyone kept their head low as they ran to the helicopter while the blades spun overhead.

The EC-155 lifted off the ramp, and as soon as they cleared the airport, it headed to the Waimea airport as fast as it would fly, which took about 10 minutes.

After landing in Waimea, Bob shut down the engines, but stayed inside the chopper ready to go whenever Sam gave the signal.

❦

As soon as Ivan Volkoff spotted the police officer heading toward the plane, he pulled out a knife and put it to Henry's throat. He screamed out the open entry door of the small plane for the cop to back off or he would kill Henry. It was a single engine Cessna that held nine passengers. Besides Ivan, Henry, and the crew, there were only a couple other people onboard, and they were sitting at the back of the plane.

Volkov had been demanding, for at least ten minutes, that the pilot take off but the pilot convinced him that the plane had to be refueled first; unless he wanted to swim halfway to Maui.

When Sam, Jessica and Gabbie arrived at the airport, Gabbie was the only one with any kind of official capacity. She did the talking, after identifying herself as an FBI agent, to the young rookie patrolman who was the responding officer. He was young, but he wasn't stupid and readily accepted Gabbie's help in trying to negotiate the release of Henry.

"Where's your backup?" Gabbie asked.

"They're all at a standoff over in Honokaa. Some drunk has barricaded himself inside his house and is threatening to kill his wife and kids. So they sent me to see if this was another false alarm since we've had multiple false sightings concerning this Amber Alert. The sarge thought this was probably another one; he sent me and another unit but they got a flat tire, it's just me."

·ª·

"There's no way you're leaving here with Henry," Gabbie yelled, from about fifty feet away from the open door of the plane sitting on the ramp.

"Even if we were to let you leave, there would be an army of cops waiting for you on Maui. The only play you have is to let Henry go and turn yourself over to us. If you do that, we will protect you from the mob. For your safety, we will fly you to the mainland today. All you have to do is walk over to that helicopter. It will take you to the airport where a jet is waiting to take you to the FBI office in Los Angeles."

Ivan knew he was screwed no matter what. After forty-five minutes of back and forth with Gabbie, he agreed to let Henry go at the bottom of the stairs of the commuter plane. Henry ran to the outstretched, waiting arms of Sam and Jessica as they knelt down together to pick him up.

Gabbie and the rookie patrolman were hustling toward Volkov to put the cuffs on him, when they heard the loud pop of a high-powered rifle in the distance. Ivan fell to the ground right there. He laid in a growing pool of blood, dead from a single bullet to his head which looked like a melon that had exploded.

They had no idea who fired the shot or where it came from or if Jessica would be the next target.

Sam and Jessica ran for the chopper as Sam carried Henry. He raised his right hand in the air spinning his index finger in a circular motion to signal Bob to spin up the helicopter's turbine engines.

❧

FROM A GRASSY CINDER CONE a half a mile away, with a 50-caliber sniper rifle, Alexei Dmitrievich made a hard, but not an impossible shot. While the million dollar reward from Sam and Jessica would have been a nice bonus, Dmitrievich's job was to kill Ivan Volkov, and that's exactly what he did.

The text he got leading him to Volkov was all he needed to put him in the ground once and for all.

31

A untie May was waiting at the house when Sam and Jessica arrived back home with Henry. She and Uncle Jack were having coffee and talking story about old times at the Aloha Village when they walked in the front door.

"Welcome home, Henry," Auntie May and Uncle Jack said in unison as the little guy clung to Jessica's shoulder. Henry cracked a brief smile and then turned his head into Jessica's neck.

She carried Henry down the hall to the bathtub to wash off the stink. It was obvious he hadn't been bathed since Volkov had abducted him.

Thirty minutes later, Jessica came down the hall, back to the dining room, where everyone was gathered. After giving Henry a bath, she had put him in his pajamas to make sure he didn't get cold. The past few nights had been chilly; a cold breeze had blown into Kona from off the top of a snowy Mauna Kea.

Jessica looked at Sam, smiling. "I detoxed him, he's safe to touch now. It's your turn, she said. He wants you to read him a bedtime story."

Sam excused himself from the dining room table and went down the hallway to Henry's room to read him a story.

Auntie May had gone in the kitchen to make a late dinner for everyone; she was busy broiling fresh fish.

Jessica sat down at the table across from Uncle Jack, and to his surprise, she said, "Now, what did the governor want me to do?"

"That's what I like about you, you don't beat around the bush. The governor needs your serial killer expertise."

"I don't know. I'm exhausted after this ordeal, and I will be taking care of Henry."

"The governor says you can take some time to think about it. And if you don't take the job, he's got somebody else in mind. But I think you should consider taking a breather and think about this for two reasons. One, there's been a lot of young women disappear over the last fifteen years on the Big Island, and nobody seems to have a clue why. Your experience, hunting two of the most vicious serial killers in California history, makes you more qualified than anybody else in Hawaii for the job." Uncle Jack paused for a second to get a piece of gum out of his pocket and then continued.

"And the second reason, this one's a biggie. Do you remember those Russian bastards on their way here to kill you?"

"You have such a way with words, Uncle." Jessica pulled out her Glock and sat it on the table. "Yes, as a matter of fact I do."

"The minute word gets out they have hired you on at the sheriff's department, the mob contract will get canceled. They won't touch you if you go back on the job. That's a bridge they can't cross and they know it."

Jessica nodded her head. She knew he was right. The only sure way she would get out of this thing alive is if she went back into law enforcement.

❧

JESSICA WONDERED why Auntie May was there talking story with Uncle Jack when they got home, but she was too frazzled to ask about it at the time. Later that night lying in bed, Sam told her he asked Auntie May if she could come help out for a while.

At that point it was obvious Jessica would sign on with the sheriff's department. And the idea of starting a private investigation firm was no longer feasible now that the mob had a contract out on her.

Auntie May had raised six kids while working at Aloha Village, and Jessica was more than happy to have the extra help from a true expert. While Jessica had raised her two younger sisters, after the death of their mother, Henry was a boy. She decided since Auntie May had raised all boys, maybe she could provide valuable insight into the workings of the mind of a young boy who thought eating his own boogers was a delicacy.

❧

SECURITY WAS STILL tight around Sam and Jessica's home at Keauhou Bay. The blinds on all the windows were closed to keep any snipers from being able to take a shot.

When Jessica woke up the next morning and couldn't see the ocean because of the blinds being closed, she made up her mind right then and there. The first thing she did after having a cup of coffee with Sam was to call Uncle Jack.

"I don't need a month. Tell the governor I'll be ready to start in a couple of days, after I get Henry stashed with Auntie May at Aloha Village."

"You sure about that, don't you want to take some time with Henry first?"

"There is no time that is safe until I deal with this."

A few hours later Uncle Jack buckled Henry's seat belt into his old Bronco. There was something funny about the little guy, everyone liked him. Even Uncle Jack, who was known for his dislike of anyone under the age of thirty-five. Uncle Jack's dog, Boomer, was in the back seat. The top of the Bronco was off and everyone's hair blew in the wind as they cruised down the highway toward Aloha Village. Boomer was a Giant Schnauzer, with black curly hair, and had the disposition of an alligator. Even he liked Henry.

§

EARLIER THAT MORNING Gabbie had taken a kayak and paddled around the bay to get some exercise and breathe in the salt air. It was rejuvenating to both her body and mind. She had experienced nothing like it before in her life. Everything had been a blur since yesterday. She and Jessica hadn't had time yet to talk about the events of the day before. Gabbie kept wondering: how did the Russians know where Volkov was? And who tipped them off? It didn't take a rocket scientist to figure out that a fifty-caliber sniper rifle had been used to kill Volkov. They didn't bring one with them, or did they? These things were a mystery to Gabbie, and when she got back to the house she and Jessica needed to talk about them. It was more out of curiosity than anything else. She was fine with the Waimea PD investigating Volkov's death and figured it would just stay on the books as an unsolved murder for a millennium.

§

JESSICA BROUGHT two cups of coffee from the kitchen to the dining room table. Gabbie was checking her email. The blinds were closed, blocking the view of the bay, and any potential snipers. Sam had gone down to the boatyard to meet with a potential new client who was ready to spend a couple hundred million on a yacht, but wouldn't commit until she met with him first.

"How can you drink that?" Jessica asked Gabbie, after watching her ruin a perfectly good cup of Kona coffee with what looked like a pound of sugar and half a cup of cream.

"It's yummy, you should try it sometime." Gabbie stirred the mixture to just shy of being like syrup.

"To each his own, I guess," Jessica conceded. "While you were still dealing with the crime scene last night, Uncle Jack told me the governor of Hawaii has a job he wants me to take." Gabbie continued to stir her coffee as she listened.

"He wants me to join a task force that's being set up to investigate a string of missing women. There is speculation it might be the work of a serial killer here on the island. Young women have been going missing here for at least fifteen years and nobody's been willing to do anything about it until now."

"So are you saying you're going back on the job?" Gabbie asked, just before taking a sip of her coffee.

Jessica's face twisted up like she had bitten into a lemon as she watched Gabbie bring the cup to her lips.

"Yes, I'm being hired at the rank of lieutenant. I know we had talked about doing private investigation, but there's no way I can do that with this mob thing hanging over me right now. I want you to think about coming to work with me at the sheriff's department. That is, if you're still planning on retiring from the FBI and moving to the island. I can make it a prerequisite for taking the job. They hire me, they hire you. What do you think?"

"I'm in." And they clinked their coffee cups together. Then Gabbie said, "Who do you think popped Volkov?"

"Honestly? I thought you tipped off the Russians, and they did it."

Gabbie frowned. "I thought you did it."

Both of the women looked at each other and at the same time, said, "Sam."

Jessica said, "Do we care?"

"Nope."

And they clinked their coffee cups together again.

Jessica reached for her phone sitting on the table. "It's time I called Larry Black and let him in on the good news about my new job."

32

L arry Black hung up the phone after talking with Jessica. He leaned back in his chair and breathed a sigh of relief. Now all he had to do was call Alina Evanoff. Once she knew that Jessica was going to work for the sheriff's department at the request of the governor of Hawaii, Larry was certain Alina would call off the hit.

"I don't care if she's a cop now, Larry. She must be dealt with because she's a threat to our operation." Those were the last words Alina said to Larry before she hung up the phone.

No matter which way it played out, it was bad for Larry. He was making millions on both sides of the fence, Alina with money laundering and Sam with commissions from super yacht sales that Larry had brokered. He would have to pick a side and hope it didn't get him killed or locked up in prison.

Alina was a new kind of mobster. She had risen quickly in the ranks to the top of the mob in Australia by murdering anyone who got in her way.

Killing cops was taboo to her predecessors. But Alina had no such fear and wasn't concerned with the ramifications of putting out a contract on a cop. The money laundering business in Hawaii was making her hundreds of millions of dollars per year and she wasn't going to let one person get in the way of that—no matter who they were.

And besides, this was personal since Jessica had screwed up Alina's plan to put Volkov back to work hacking banks.

The thought of Jessica bringing an investigation into Alina's money laundering business was too great a threat to ignore. Jessica must die.

❦

DAVE WHITEHOUSE WAS the best sales consultant Stewart Super Yachts had, but there was no way he would close the deal with Ms. Nastya Borisova. Not without a face-to-face meeting with Sam Stewart. She made it clear, if Mr. Stewart couldn't be bothered, she'd take her business elsewhere.

Dave had been working with Ms. Borisova for a few days and she wanted to have a yacht built that would rival Paul Allen's, the co-owner of Microsoft. His biggest yacht, the Octopus, was one of the largest in the world, and Ms. Borisova wanted a bigger one to add to her collection.

Sam arrived at the boatyard to meet Ms. Borisova. She wasn't what he was expecting, to say the least.

She wore a platinum blonde wig with a low cut, skimpy black dress and an undersized pushup bra; with a thousand-dollar pair of Manolo Blahnik snakeskin, pointy toe pumps. The snakeskin shoes were a sign of her true nature. *Distracting* would have been an understatement of the ensemble she was wearing.

Nastya Borisova was one of Alina Evanoff's aliases and she had a whole closet full of wigs for whoever she wanted to be that day. She had a phony company setup for each alias she assumed. There was plenty of money in the bank to persuade anyone who bothered to check her ability to spend hundreds of millions of dollars on a yacht or anything else for that matter.

Ms. Borisova was in Sam's office sitting in his chair when he walked through the door.

"How can I help you, Ms. Borisova? No, no, don't get up. I might sell you the company," Sam joked. She and Sam both fake laughed to ease the moment of tension. If she was serious about spending millions of dollars with Sam's company, she could sit anywhere she wanted as far as he was concerned.

"I don't spend over a million dollars on anything without meeting the principle of the company," she said, in perfect English.

Sam sat down on the couch, off to the side of his desk, because the chairs in front hurt his back. "I don't either," he said.

She got up, came over and sat next to him, crossed her long legs and swiveled her hips toward Sam so he could see the whole package up close and personal.

"Your Mr. Whitehouse is an excellent representative of your company. But if I'm going to put down a deposit for ten million to start construction, I'm going to personally hand the check to you, Mr. Stewart."

Sam couldn't help but enjoy the sweet aroma of her expensive perfume swirling in his nostrils. But it was the ten million he wanted more than anything else. When it came to money, Sam never took his eye off the ball. And the check was the ball.

"I'll be happy to accept your check, Ms. Borisova."

"I don't have it here now, but if we meet for dinner tonight, I'll be sure to bring it with me."

Sam shifted his body toward her on the couch. "How about noon tomorrow at the Marlin House at Aloha Village? Of course I'll be bringing my wife Jessica. Our son has been staying with his Auntie out there during the makahiki festival."

Ms. Borisova smiled. "Of course, I love a good threesome. And maybe I'll get to meet your son."

She and Sam stood up, and she squeezed his hand just before turning to leave.

After she left, Sam stopped by Dave Whitehouse's office and stuck his head in the door. "She says she's bringing a check for ten million tomorrow at lunch. Dig up everything you can on her." Dave interrupted, "I checked all her financials, her bank says she's got the money to make the check good."

Sam nodded okay. "That's why you're my best guy, Dave." And he left the office to go back home and let Jessica know that he needed her to come with him the next day for a lunch meeting with Ms. Borisova.

᠊᠊᠊᠊᠊

GABBIE DIDN'T LIKE it one bit when she got wind of Jessica planning to go to lunch the next day at the Marlin House with Sam. It had been a few days since Jessica had been outside and she was tired of waiting to find out for sure if the contract had been canceled. The bug in Larry's office had quit working, so that was a no go for any kind of intel. At least until Gabbie could figure out a way to get back in his office, without him being there, and plant another bug.

It was true that Jessica had said it was all good between her and Larry because of his tip, about where Volkov was, when they were searching frantically for Henry. But Gabbie had no such arrangement with him. If she could gather enough evidence to have Larry indicted for anything, that would be her mission until she retired and went to work with Jessica at the sheriff's department.

The next day Gabbie insisted on going along to the lunch meeting. She told Sam in no uncertain terms, "I'll be sitting at a table nearby or she isn't going." Sam agreed and at 11:15

a.m. they got in the armored Tahoe parked inside the garage and headed out to the Marlin House.

"It's nice to get out of the house and go have lunch out in public like normal people," Jessica remarked, as they pulled out of the driveway.

They were maybe a hundred yards from the driveway when a barrage of gunfire peppered the side of the Tahoe.

Viktor Zinchenko and his crew had planned Jessica's hit with the same precision they used when they snatched Volkov from Homeland Security. But the one thing they didn't know was that the Tahoe was armored. Or that it had a 6.2 liter supercharged engine and would easily outrun their rental van. And the other thing was that Jessica knew all the roads and they didn't.

Jessica had fired a couple rounds out of the window at the pursuing vehicle to slow them down.

"Stop, I'll drive!" Jessica yelled at Sam, while the bullets were ricocheting off of the SUV. Sam slid out of the way and Jessica got behind the wheel and floored it, laying sixty feet of rubber as the heavy Tahoe started to gain momentum. There was so much smoke in the air, it temporarily blinded Zinchenko and his men. She ran the light at Alii Drive and Kam lll and turned right heading south.

The last thing Jessica wanted was a shootout with those guys. Zinchenko's men outnumbered them and they were pros. The best option was to try and lose them. By the time the tire smoke had cleared and Zinchenko and his crew got in their van to give chase, they couldn't see which way the Tahoe turned at the intersection down the street. They guessed wrong and turned left.

It was too dangerous to drive any further than they had to. The only place Sam and Jessica knew where a helicopter could land nearby was at the Kona hospital. Sam called his new chopper pilot, Bob, and told him to pick them up there as soon as possible.

By the time they arrived at the hospital Bob was a half a mile out and on a vector to the landing pad.

After everyone was onboard the helicopter, Jessica got a text from Uncle Jack.

"I've got intel from my source at Homeland Security that says the plane Sam told to return to Australia didn't and continued on to Kona. The Russians on board told the pilot if they landed back in Gold Coast they would kill him and not to change course."

Jessica texted Uncle Jack.

"Thanks, we've already met them. We're in the chopper on the way to the airport."

"Do you want me to meet you somewhere?"

Uncle Jack replied.

"Yes, meet us at the airport. Sam says he needs your help."

33

As the Eurocopter was on its way to the airport, Sam was seated far enough away from Jessica and Gabbie that they couldn't hear him talking on his phone when he called Alexei Dmitrievich.

"Are your guys still there with you?" Sam asked.

"Konechno."

Annoyed, Sam asked, "What does that mean in English?"

"It means "of course," Dmitrievich said, with a thick Russian accent.

"Is that better Mr. Stewart?"

"How would you like to make another million?"

"Who do we have to kill?" Dmitrievich said half joking.

"Viktor Zinchenko."

There was a long silence on the phone before Dmitrievich answered. "Make it five million because he will be hard to kill."

"Three," Sam countered.

"Three point five and we'll dispose of the bodies like they were never here."

"Do it," Sam said.

There was no love between the two mob factions, and the

money was good, so Dmitrievich had no problem with the job.

In the meantime the chopper had just flown over Kailua Bay. It was heading toward the airport when Jessica tapped Gabbie's leg to get her attention. Gabbie had been looking out the opposite window at the old church in the village below and was mesmerized by the beauty of the village from the air.

"That's the *Akula* anchored in the bay. What do you want to bet that bitch that tried to kill us is onboard?" Jessica said.

Gabbie nodded in agreement.

WHEN THE CHOPPER sat down at the airport, Sam wanted to go get Henry and leave the island until Dmitrievich and his crew could handle the situation. Jessica wasn't having any part of that idea. The thought of Sam having paid to fly those mercenaries to the island pissed her off even more, and she had every intention of making Alina Evanoff pay the price for it.

"That's fine, honey. Why don't you take Henry to Bullhead City and see Uncle Frank until this is over. I'm going to find this Alina Evanoff, or whatever her name is, and I will cuff her or kill her. It'll be her choice."

Sam had always been the alpha in the room but Jessica was having no part of that. Her father had raised her to take control of her destiny, and this was a prime example of when she would do just that.

Uncle Jack was waiting at the hanger when the chopper got there. He was well armed and ready to do whatever Sam and Jessica needed him to do. On that day he would escort Sam to Aloha Village to get Henry and then head back to the airport, where Mike Thompson would be waiting to take off in the company jet for Bullhead City, Arizona.

The chopper sat on the ground at the airport just long

enough for Jessica and Gabbie to get out and Uncle Jack to get in, then it lifted off for Aloha Village.

Uncle Jack had parked his old Bronco next to the hanger by Air Services, and the key was under the floor mat where he said it would be. The Bronco had a built-in gun safe in the bed; and there were two AR-15's with five hundred rounds. If Jessica and Gabbie crossed paths with Viktor Zinchenko, and company, they would be prepared.

Jessica and Gabbie headed to the harbor to get the charter boat Sam kept there. Most of the time he loaned the *Fish Hunter* out to his rich friends visiting from the mainland. But this month it was out of service because it just had two new engines installed. Sam would let no one but him or Jessica drive the boat until the new engines were properly broken in; they were MAN marine engines at a cost of two hundred and fifty-thousand each.

"Why are we going to the harbor?" Gabbie asked.

"Because we're going to take one of our other boats to Kailua Bay and see if that bitch, Alina Evanoff, is on board the *Akula*."

"Oh, this should be fun," Gabbie said. She turned her head to look at the coast as they headed toward the harbor—and possibly their own deaths.

34

The chopper was thirty seconds from landing at Aloha Village, when Sam told Bob to abort and return to the airport. As the helicopter was making a sweeping high right turn Sam asked Uncle Jack, "Has she been this stubborn her whole life?"

"You could call it that, I think. When she sets her mind to do something, that's it," Uncle Jack answered.

When they landed at the airport Sam and Uncle Jack took a golf cart over to Sam's Gulfstream jet. "I thought you were staying?" Uncle Jack questioned Sam.

"I am, I just need to get something out of the plane."

Uncle Jack sat in the golf cart and waited until Sam exited the plane and got back in the cart. He brought with him a large duffle bag and placed it in the back of the cart behind the seat.

"What's in the bag?"

"Two AR-15's, and a couple hundred rounds. A couple of Glocks with loaded spare clips. Duct tape, knives, canvas tarp. Stuff like that."

"Almost sounds like a murder kit," Uncle Jack said.

"I just like to be prepared when I travel to some less secure countries," Sam said.

Bob started the engines of the helicopter but shut them down right away when an oil temperature light came on.

"No worries, Bob, get it checked out and we'll get a rental car to run out to the village and back," Sam said.

While they waited for the rental company to deliver a vehicle, Sam called Jessica.

When she answered the phone, the first thing she asked was, "Are you airborne?"

"No, I couldn't leave you here to deal with this alone."

"I'm not alone, I'm with Gabbie. We have guns and a lot of ammunition. Your idea to go get Henry and take him to the mainland was the right choice to make. If we both get killed, as in you and I, Henry is once again an orphan. Now go get him and get your ass on the plane and get the hell off this island until I call you and say it's safe to come back."

Sam looked at Uncle Jack after he hung up the phone. "Add bossy to her description, too."

Uncle Jack smiled. "What did she say?"

"That I should get my ass on the plane with Henry so he's not orphaned again."

"So what are you going to do?"

Sam sighed, "She's right. I need to go get Henry and take him to the mainland until this is all over and it's safe to come back."

35

As Jessica and Gabbie rounded Kaiwi Point on the *Fish Hunter*, they still had no idea how they would get on board the *Akula*. That was until Jessica spotted the parasail boat about half a mile away towing a couple of tourists high above the ocean in a tandem parachute harness.

Jessica changed course from Kailua Bay and turned the *Fish Hunter* toward the parasail boat. She pushed the throttles forward to increase the power to the combined sixteen hundred horsepower engines. It only took a few minutes to catch up to the parasail boat heading away from them.

When the parasail boat had come to a stop, Jessica pulled alongside as they were switching customers out of the parachute. She made the boat's captain an offer he couldn't refuse. Finish the charter was all he had to do, then Jessica would charter the boat for the rest of the day and buy one new parachute.

Once they had a deal, she and Gabbie met the parasail boat captain back at the pier so he could drop off his customers and they could tie up the *Fish Hunter*.

Jessica and Gabbie would board the parasail boat and

head back out toward the middle of the bay where the *Akula* was.

"Let's do a drive-by and see if there's anyone on deck but keep going until we get out a half mile or so," Jessica told the captain.

Jessica was wearing a big sun hat and sunglasses. She looked just like any other tourist passing by in case there was anyone on deck that might recognize her.

"Not too close," she said, as the parasail boat captain neared the stern of the *Akula*.

Jessica couldn't believe it when she saw Larry Black on deck talking to a woman who matched the description Sam gave of Nastya Borisova. She was wearing a platinum blonde wig. It had to be her. She and Larry appeared to be alone topside having a heated discussion about something. While she couldn't hear what they were saying, Larry's animated movements showed that he wasn't happy about something.

Jessica looked at Gabbie and said, "Hopefully 'murder-for-hire' isn't with them down below deck."

Gabbie nodded and reminded Jessica she didn't think this was a great idea, but agreed she had nothing better to offer.

When Jessica had seen enough, she tapped the captain on the shoulder and motioned for him to speed up and turn away from the *Akula*.

Once they were about a half a mile away, she and Gabbie got into the tandem parachute harness and lifted off the rear of the parachute boat. There was a strong headwind and they were quickly airborne. The captain pressed the winch control button to let line out at a hundred feet a minute. Minutes later Jessica and Gabbie were at four hundred feet above the ocean. The only thing they could hear was the wind ruffling the panels in the parachute above their heads.

"Wow, look at the view! We should do this sometime just for fun… if we don't get killed," Gabbie said.

Jessica cut her eyes over with a look of disapproval.

"You have to be more positive, Gabbie."

"I'm *positive* we could get killed today," Gabbie said. Jessica just shook her head.

All Jessica could do was focus on the landing atop of the helo deck of the *Akula*. Unlike Gabbie, who liked to crack jokes in the face of death, Jessica was all business that day.

Down below on the parasail boat, the captain waved his hat to signal that they had reached the spot where he would come around one hundred and eighty degrees. That would put the parachute canopy straight into the wind, allowing him to place Jessica and Gabbie exactly where he wanted to. It was perfect conditions. A stiff breeze made the chute just hang in the air before setting them down right in the middle of the helicopter deck.

Jessica was more worried about crashing into the super-structure of the yacht and dying from that, than she was of Alina's hit squad that may or may not be on board.

The only comforting thing about it was, that over the years, she had watched the parasail boat captain carefully dip tourists in the water just before bringing them back on board at the end of their ride.

She assumed if he was that good then he could put them right on the yacht's helicopter landing pad. And she figured right. He put them down right in the middle where "X" marks the spot on the deck.

She and Gabbie unbuckled their harnesses as fast as they could before getting dragged over the side of the boat by a gust of wind.

The helo deck was forward of the bridge. There would be no sneaking on board for sure.

Jessica and Gabbie acted like tourists who had been the victims of an incompetent boat operator. Two crew members of the *Akula* came running to see if they were okay.

Larry and Alina were no longer at the stern of the boat and had moved inside before Jessica and Gabbie had landed.

Gabbie didn't waste any time before trying to pump the crew for information. "We heard this beautiful yacht belongs to a Russian billionaire."

The younger of the two crew members started to answer and the more senior one interrupted him. "We are not allowed to disclose anything about the owner. I'm sorry," he said, in broken English.

"I'm sorry, too," Gabbie replied. She then pulled her Glock and told them to have a seat on the deck, while she hand-cuffed them to the railing.

While Gabbie was handcuffing the two crew members, Jessica ran toward the rear of the boat. She knew Alina was inside and it was time for them to meet.

36

One of Dmitrievich's men was a spy for Zinchenko, and was relaying every move of Dmitrievich and his crew, so Zinchenko and his team could set up an ambush.

Zinchenko had expanded his crew by four that day. After he killed Dmitrievich and his top lieutenant, Nikita Gorev, before going to Aloha Village, the remaining soldiers of Dmitrievich were only loyal to the dollar, and hired on with Zinchenko right there on the spot. It was either that —or die.

&

SAM AND UNCLE JACK pulled into the parking lot at Aloha Village. "They're here! How the hell did they know...?" Sam's voice trailed off while he pointed at a brown rental van that had a couple of bullet holes in it. Then he continued, "Jessica put those there just after we left the house and they attacked us in the Tahoe."

Then it dawned on Sam. "Borisova had to have been Alina Evanoff, and she told them we would be here at noon." Sam shook his head; he couldn't believe that he had been duped by her. And not only that, but he had led them straight to Henry.

Uncle Jack pulled his Glock and racked the slide to chamber a round. He held the pistol with his left hand, and had it parked on top of his lap, pointed toward the car door; to be ready if need be.

"Let's just be cool; park here and hang tight for a minute."

Uncle Jack called his connection at HSI for help and gave him the GPS coordinates of the resort's location so HSI could send help as soon as possible. After he got off the phone, he and Sam sneaked down to the beach to see where Zinchenko and his men were.

Homeland Security in Honolulu wanted payback for the embarrassment they had suffered. They were willing to pull out all the stops to catch the Russian team responsible for Volkov's abduction. They had a SWAT team airborne on an Army Blackhawk helicopter twenty minutes after Uncle Jack called them.

The small resort was eerily quiet; Zinchenko and his men had rounded up all the staff and tourists staying at the twelve-bungalow resort. They were holding them at gunpoint inside the Marlin House restaurant, and were trying to figure out which kid, among the group of preschoolers there, was Henry.

That day at the village, the staff had planned to release sea turtles on the beach and had invited a local preschool class to come and participate. They were all having lunch inside the restaurant when Zinchenko and his men stormed in and told everyone to get on the floor and shut up.

Uncle Jack and Sam had spotted an armed guard outside of the Marlin House. Uncle Jack figured the SWAT team was at least twenty minutes away from touching down at the village. They had no other choice than to wait until help arrived since they were outnumbered. They hid in a secluded spot, overlooking the beach and the Marlin House, where it gave them a good vantage point until help could arrive.

When Sam looked through his binoculars and saw all the kids, along with Auntie May and Henry, being held inside that changed everything.

He was starting to make a move when Uncle Jack grabbed his arm. "Wait. They'll kill you and not think twice about it. This is one time we have to wait, since we are way outnumbered."

Sam cut his eyes toward the dive boat tied off close to the beach. "We need a diversion to get them away from the hostages. I'll turn the boat into a giant Molotov cocktail and then swim out of the bay and come back ashore. When they run down to the beach to check it out you cut them down."

A lot of bad things could happen before HSI arrived on scene, and Uncle Jack thought Sam's plan was better than waiting to find out. Sam kept the Russians under surveillance while Uncle Jack sneaked back to the car. When he got to the car he grabbed both of the AR-15's and the duffle bag from the plane and hurried back into position.

There was only one small problem, neither of them smoked and had no way to start a fire. But there was a guard posted outside the restaurant; Sam and Uncle Jack had noticed the man light one cigarette after another while he stood guard.

"We need his lighter," Sam said.

"What do you propose, we walk up and ask him for a light?" Uncle Jack joked.

"Something like that. I'll swim out along the shoreline; come around on his flank, drag his ass in the bushes and ask to borrow his lighter."

Sam swam two miles in the ocean three to four times a week; he could swim the distance no problem. But doing it and not getting spotted might prove to be a difficult thing to pull off.

Sam needed to swim a couple hundred yards north of the beach. From where he and Uncle Jack were hiding, it would be easy for the guard to spot Sam entering the water at the beach. He would have to hike down the coastline, south of the beach, and enter the surf out of sight of the Marlin House and the guard. Then he'd swim back past the mouth of the bay and come ashore on the north side of the resort.

The best chance he had would be to hold his breath as long as he could, while swimming under the surface as far as he could, as he swam past the bay. And only surface to grab a breath and hopefully not get spotted or shot in the process.

37

J essica found Alina Evanoff following Larry Black out to the rear pool deck yelling at him as he walked away from her. "You take orders from me now. It's not like the old days. Now I tell you, you don't tell me, remember that!"

Larry had his back to Jessica as he looked over the rail of the *Akula* toward Kailua village a few hundred yards away. He didn't see her as she approached them. But Alina saw her and stopped yelling at Larry and charged towards Jessica. She leapt into the air with a side kick, which Jessica sidestepped and only suffered a glancing blow.

Jessica spun around with a roundhouse kick and caught Alina on the chin and knocked her down. Alina was tough, most people would have been knocked out from a kick like that. She spat blood and smiled. "Is that all you got, bitch?"

"Oh no, honey, I'm just warming up," Jessica said, as she rotated her neck to loosen up.

Jessica went into her fighting stance. She could have pulled her Glock, but first she would beat Alina to a pulp and then cuff her. She needed some satisfaction.

Alina went into her Russian martial arts stance known as

Systema. The KGB had trained her in the martial arts before the collapse of the Soviet Union.

Jessica was facing Alina when she heard Larry rack the slide of his 380 semi-auto he had in his pocket. Jessica took her eyes off of Alina for a split second but it was too late. Alina connected a side kick to the side of Jessica's head; this time she went down hard and Alina followed up with a kick to the ribcage.

Jessica was on her hands and knees trying to get back on her feet but Alina's kick had almost knocked her out.

That bitch kicks like a mule was her first thought. The second thought was *why was Larry chambering a round?*

"Loser dies," Larry said.

Alina leapt forward and was going to kick Jessica again, when Larry pointed his pistol at her and said, "If you kick her while she's down, I'll shoot you."

That extra few seconds was all Jessica needed to start to get back on her feet. Larry put the gun down at his side; Alina relaunched her attack and leapt forward with a short kick to the ribs as Jessica was trying to get up. That kick connected and knocked her back down.

Jessica hadn't been in the dojo in a few months and it showed. But unlike the Karate Kid, there would be no rematch here.

Out of the corner of her eye Jessica glimpsed Gabbie being held at gunpoint by half a dozen members of the yacht's crew.

One thing at a time she thought to herself, as she got back to her feet. Alina charged again but this time Jessica was ready for her. She gave Alina an upper cut into her stomach on the right side and then a haymaker coming over the left to her head, as she bent over from the gut punch. Alina went down and was out cold.

Larry ejected the round out of his gun, picked it up and put it back in the magazine. He then put the pistol back in his pocket. "I was kidding. I wouldn't shoot the loser, I just thought it was motivation for a good cat fight."

Jessica glared at him as she put the handcuffs on Alina. Larry told the crew in Russian to release Gabbie. They followed his orders and gave her gun back to her.

When Alina regained consciousness, she was not happy about being handcuffed. She rolled over, sat up and screamed at Larry in Russian that she would get him; and that she had always thought he was a loser in the KGB.

Larry looked down at her and answered her rant in their native tongue. "You're lucky, if we were in the old country I'd put a bullet in your head right here, right now."

Jessica and Gabbie understood that Alina and Larry were pissed off at each other but that was about it since neither one of them were fluent in Russian.

What they didn't know was Uncle Jack urged his friends at Homeland Security to have Navy SEALs pay a visit to the *Akula* in the middle of the night. The SEALs were on temporary assigned duty aboard the Coast Guard cutter anchored in Kailua Bay earlier in the week. Their mission was to plant listening devices on the outside decks, near the pool, where they had noticed large gatherings of visitors to the yacht on a regular basis.

Uncle Jack wasn't fluent in Russian, but he understood enough of it to get the gist of what Alina and Larry had said, when they were yelling at each other. Later that day he shared the information with Jessica and Gabbie.

꙯

Agents from Homeland Security and the FBI arrived from Oahu and boarded the *Akula*.

HSI agents took Alina into custody and transported her to the Federal detention center in Honolulu.

"You better get back in the dojo. I thought she was going to kick your ass there for a minute," Gabbie laughed.

Jessica reached over and rubbed her bruised ribs. "I think you're right about the dojo. But lose to that bitch? Never happen."

"While you're in the dojo getting back in shape, I'll be filing my retirement papers and getting my things packed to move to Kona. Because after my boss finds out about the shenanigans I've been up to, I'll be lucky if they don't fire me instead of letting me retire."

38

Sam swam underwater most of the way across the mouth of the bay and only had to come up for air a few times. He was lucky not to get spotted. One time the guard had glanced in Sam's direction just as he was ducking down after taking a breath. The guard noticed the ripples in the water but brushed it off as a turtle or a fish.

After swimming a couple hundred yards past the bay, Sam climbed up the rocky shoreline so he could flank the guard. Sam sneaked through the jungle behind the Marlin House, all the while being careful not to make any noise.

It would be difficult to snatch the guard without being seen by someone looking out a window of the restaurant.

The only way that would work would be to draw the guard into the thick vegetation and take him out without being seen by the others inside the restaurant.

Sam tossed a rock towards the guard and when he came to investigate, he jumped him and put him out with a chokehold after threes seconds. After the guard was unconscious, he taped his mouth shut. He then wrapped the guard's arms around a coconut tree and secured them by wrapping tape around the guard's wrists.

Sam grabbed the lighter out of the guard's shirt pocket, put it in a waterproof bag, and stuffed it in the pocket of his shorts before sneaking back the way he had come. After making his way back to the shoreline through the jungle, he entered the surf and swam back to the dive boat. It was the only way to make it to the dive boat without being spotted.

From the mouth of the bay to the dive boat was about two hundred yards, and with only a couple of breaths, Sam managed to swim most of the way underwater.

Uncle Jack had been waiting and watching for Sam. When he saw him start to climb up over the side of the dive boat he aimed his rifle at the doorway of the Marlin House.

Sam got on board the dive boat without being spotted by anyone besides Uncle Jack. He found a towel, shredded it with his pocket knife, and used it as the fuse for the Molotov cocktail he was going to turn the boat into.

Sam stuck the improvised fuse into the filler pipe for the gas tank and lit it. Then he jumped overboard and started swimming for the beach, a hundred yards away, as fast as he could.

If Sam's calculation, which was a wild-ass guess, was right, he had just enough time to get back to the high ground with Uncle Jack before the boat exploded.

The fuse burned faster than Sam expected. He barely made it to the beach when the dive boat exploded. It turned into an orange ball of flames in the small bay. Minutes later black smoke billowed from the remains of the boat and flames engulfed the rest.

THE THICK SMOKE started blowing toward the Marlin House when the wind shifted. Zinchenko stayed inside while all of his men poured out of the restaurant to see what had happened.

He let no one escape the toxic smoke, as it started to fill the open air restaurant, while he stood near the doorway holding his shirt over his nose and mouth with one hand and holding a pistol in the other.

One tourist, a middle-aged man, tried to run out the front door and Zinchenko shot him before he got to it.

Uncle Jack had picked off four of Zinchenko's men as they ran out to see what had blown up.

"Cover me," Sam yelled, as he ran down the beach toward the Marlin House with his rifle. Uncle Jack laid down suppression fire and had the remaining Russians pinned down behind a canoe shed near the restaurant.

The Russians couldn't establish a line of fire toward Sam as he ran past them to the restaurant—Uncle Jack was keeping them busy.

Zinchenko made a run for it through a back door and into the jungle as the HSI Blackhawk helicopter came on the scene. As he escaped through the jungle, he found and freed his comrade that Sam had bound to the coconut tree.

The SWAT team fast-roped down a line hanging from the chopper as it hovered above the Marlin House. From their vantage point on top of the building, the SWAT team took out the Russians hiding behind the canoe house.

As much as Sam wanted to go after Zinchenko, saving Henry was his only mission.

Zinchenko and his last remaining soldier had made it to their rental van and were making a run for the highway a mile away. The Black Hawk caught up to them as the van swerved all over the dirt road, at a high rate of speed as they tried to escape.

Zinchenko's man leaned out of the passenger side window and fired his AK-47 toward the Black Hawk.

The door gunner of the Black Hawk opened up on him with its M-240 machine gun. Zinchenko and his man were both splattered all over the inside of the van when it crashed and burned in the old lava flow that flanked the road.

ҙ

THE WIND HAD SHIFTED AGAIN from onshore to offshore, and the smoke from the dive boat was clearing from the Marlin House, as Sam ran inside to find Henry.

Auntie May and Henry were lying face down, with a group of kids on the floor, with wet towels covering their noses and mouths.

Sam snatched up Henry from the floor and held him against his shoulder with one arm. He reached down with the other to help Auntie May get up, and they hustled all the kids outside to the fresh air.

Auntie May went to calm the traumatized kids and guests while Sam took Henry and walked down the beach away from everyone. They sat down in the sand at the water's edge so Sam could check Henry out.

"Are you okay?" he asked Henry. He shook his head that he was okay as the tears began to stream down his cheeks. Sam could see the soot, from the smoke that Henry had breathed in and out, at the base of his nose. Sam carefully wiped the soot away with the towel Henry had been holding onto.

While Sam and Henry sat on the beach Uncle Jack grabbed the tarp out of Sam's duffle bag. He covered all the dead Russians so there would be no way any of the kids, including Henry, would see them as they passed by the canoe house on the way out of the village.

After everyone had left the beach, the SWAT team bagged and tagged the dead Russians and loaded them into the Blackhawk chopper. Two hours later it looked like nothing had happened that day at Aloha Village--except for the dead tourist, a dive boat blown to smithereens, and the stench of liquified fiberglass still smoldering in the bay.

39

Two weeks later.

Henry was playing fetch with Prince on the lawn behind their house at Keauhou Bay. Sam and Jessica were sitting in lawn chairs nearby, watching him when Jessica turned to Sam. "I talked to Gabbie this morning. She called when I was out paddling. They allowed her to put in her retirement papers. Multiple federal agencies had been after Alina Evanoff for about five years. And because of Gabbie's involvement, Alina will be in prison for a long time. Gabbie's bosses ignored the fact that she had gone off the reservation, they looked the other way and let her retire. She said she'll be moving here in two or three months. It just depends on how long it takes to sell her condo. And in other news, I got an email from Uncle Jack asking us to keep an eye on his boat. He said he needs to go to the mainland for a couple of weeks for some kind of training that he was very secretive about. He's thinking about coming out of retirement and going back to work for the government as an independent contractor. He said since I've been back on the island it's been like work for him and he might as well get paid for it. But he wouldn't say which agency he would work for. My guess is since it still looks like a Russian crime syndicate is operating on the island, it will be Homeland Security."

Jessica paused for a moment and took a sip of her iced tea.

"We haven't talked about me taking the job with the Sheriff's Department lately." She set her glass of tea down and turned toward Sam.

"Although all the people that wanted me dead are now themselves dead or in prison, I still need to take the job. I know you would prefer that I stay home full-time with Henry, and I would like to do that. But the bottom line is, there's a serial killer on this island hunting young women. Someone with a particular set of skills needs to do something about it, and I'm that someone."

Sam nodded. "If that's what you need to do, we'll work it out."

Jessica continued. "When Gabbie moves here she's going to be my partner. That's the deal the Governor and the Sheriff agreed to. The Sheriff didn't like my terms, but that was the only way I'd take the job."

Sam nodded again. "Do what you have to do. Henry will be okay. When you're working, Auntie May and I will take up the slack. But—and this is a big but—you still have to go see someone about your willingness to kill yourself to save Henry. I know it might sound like it was a noble gesture on your part, but I suspect there's more to it than that."

Jessica stared deep into Sam's eyes and nodded her head that she would, and then reached over and took his hand. They sat there the rest of the afternoon and watched Henry play until it was time to get ready for the luau that evening at Aloha Village.

❦

"OVER THE RAINBOW," by Brother IZ, played over the

outdoor sound system that evening when Sam, Jessica, and Henry arrived at the luau grounds at Aloha Village. Auntie May took Henry over to the group of little kids she had gathered next to the luau stage. She mesmerized the little ones with stories of how the menehune had built everything from the fishponds to the bungalows at Aloha Village. There was no doubt in the minds of each of the keiki that the menehunes were real by the end of story time with Auntie May.

Moored in the bay at Aloha Village was a new dive boat. The moonlight glistened off of its shiny gel coat. Sam's company had delivered the boat that week to replace the one he had turned into a Molotov cocktail two weeks before. The smoke damage to the Marlin House was minimal and cleaned up by the week afterward; Sam covered all the damage-related expenses.

The beach boys of Aloha Village removed the pig from the imu after it had been cooking for the previous eight hours; it was served for dinner that evening. Everyone savored the pulled pork before watching the fire knife dancers spin their flaming batons during the luau.

❧

THE NEXT MORNING at about 5:30 a.m., Sam went out to the lanai overlooking Keauhou Bay to have his morning coffee. He always used that time to think about what he would do that day. But the first thing he would do was take a pain pill. His back pain had kept him awake half the night and the other half of the night he was awake thinking about what he knew he needed to do the next day.

The birds were starting to chirp as it began to get light outside. Jessica and Henry were still asleep in the house. Sam took a sip of his coffee and sat the cup down on the table next to his chair. He reached into his pocket and pulled out the engagement ring he had been carrying since he bought it for Jessica.

He knew today was the day that he would ask her again to marry him. Technically, he already had. Even though she had agreed, he needed to do it the right way this time, because she was worth it. She deserved more than the off-the-cuff way he had asked her before.

He took another sip of coffee as he watched the early morning canoe paddlers launch their boats into the bay. It was another beautiful morning in Hawaii. His face basked in the glow of pink clouds reflecting the sun off of the water as it rose above Hualalai Mountain, behind the house.

After finishing his coffee, Sam went into the kitchen and started to prepare breakfast for Jessica and Henry.

His plan was to bring her breakfast in bed with one of the covered plates holding the engagement ring he had previously bought for her.

Sam woke Henry up and made him a bowl of cereal. He explained to him that he had a surprise later and needed his help being quiet, for the time being, because they didn't want to wake Jessica up.

Henry quietly munched on his Honey Nut Cheerios while watching Sam cook eggs in the kitchen. Prince sat beside Henry and watched him eat while being ready to pounce on any morsel that might drop his way.

After making Jessica's breakfast, Sam brought a bed tray into their room. He carefully sat the tray down at the foot of the bed. He came over and nuzzled her neck to wake her up. She opened her eyes. Sam whispered, "I've brought you breakfast."

Jessica stretched and smiled, then pushed herself up against the headboard and waited for Sam to set the breakfast tray over her lap.

"Henry's in the kitchen having breakfast, so don't worry about him," Sam said.

There were two covered plates on the tray.

"Bacon and eggs are under the left plate and something else is under the right."

Jessica started to take the lid off of the mystery food. Sam said, "Wait." And he dropped to one knee alongside of the bed.

She looked at him with confusion on her face as to what he was doing. She was still half asleep when she pulled the cover off the top of the mystery plate. There sat the most beautiful diamond engagement ring she had ever seen before. Her eyes began to tear as she looked at Sam.

Sam took hold of her hand and said, "Baby I love you, you and Henry are the most important people in my life. Will you marry me? I love you, baby."

Jessica nodded as her tears began to stream down both her cheeks.

"Okay Henry, you can come in!" Sam said.

He was waiting outside the bedroom door for the signal from Sam. Henry and Prince ran in and jumped on the bed with Jessica. They almost knocked over the breakfast tray. Sam grabbed the table and set it aside and the three of them had a group hug with Prince trying to lick all of their faces.

The End

Click here for next book notification.

AUTHOR NOTES

Aloha, mahalo (thank you) for spending your time and hard earned money on this book. I hope you enjoyed it. **If you could please post a review** on Amazon I would be very grateful.

Your review is critical to my success as an author and will help me write better books in the future. Mahalo! Click here to post review.

Thanks again,

J.E. Trent Author

ALSO BY J.E. TRENT

Book 1 Death in Paradise

In paradise nothing is simple…

…not even murder.

For Jessica, this time it's personal.

The knock at the door shook her from a deep sleep. When she saw the cops, Jessica knew why they were there. As a LA Detective, she'd been on the other side of the door plenty of times.

Someone she loved was dead.

Time slowed. Her heart sank. They knew she knew.

Before they could get to the news, her mind raced. Growing up in Hawaii, daughter to a father-in-law enforcement and a mother whose family is yakuza, she'd known the darker side of life.

As the detectives explained why they'd come, Jessica was only partly listening until they said it was her father who'd died…

…in a plane wreck.

And in that moment, the instinct to grieve was gone. He was meticulous in his maintenance. She didn't believe it was an accident.

Who murdered her father?

Jessica was going home to Hawaii.

You'll love this gripping thriller with a taste of romance, because of the twists, turns, and complex characters.

Get it now.

Book 2 Death Orchid

Book 3 Death in Hawaii Get this prequel for free when you join my email list. It's the only place it's available.- **Click here.**

ABOUT THE AUTHOR

J.E. Trent

J.E. Trent is an emerging author of Hawaii crime thrillers. The Death in Hawaii Series takes place on the Kona side of the big island of Hawaii.

J.E. Trent lived full time in Hawaii for over twenty two years and loves sharing his knowledge of the tropical paradise in his novels.

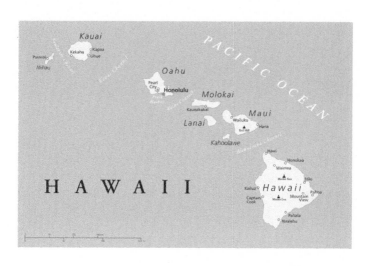

ACKNOWLEDGMENTS

A Big Mahalo to my wife, Eila, for the final edit. It was only because of her input that this story came out as well as it did. I'm truly blessed to have her kokua. (help)

Shane Rutherford at Dark Moon Graphics made the beautiful cover for the book.

Mahalo to all the authors who have shared their knowledge at kboards.com and the 20BooksTo50K Facebook group and many others.

Mahalo to my friend Capt. Steve Kaiser who has taken me deep sea fishing aboard his Cabo many times. I am indebted to him for sharing his in-depth knowledge of the sea with me. He has been a great friend for over twenty years and for that, I'm a very grateful.

   Mahalo to my friend John Masters for sharing his knowledge of deep sea fishing with me over lunch. The mere mention of his name in Hawaiian waters makes fish tremble. He's living proof you don't need a big boat, it's what you do with your pole that matters.

AFTERWORD

At the time when I got the idea for Sam and Jessica I had been an auto mechanic for about thirty-five years. I was over fifty and my body was screaming at me every morning that I'd better find another way to make a living. Around that time I had written some flash fiction that I had gotten a lot of positive feedback on and thought with some study that maybe I could write a novel.

After a lot of brainstorming, Sam and Jessica came to be. A billionaire super yacht builder and a retired LA detective. They aren't perfect; they're growing through problems in their lives that people can relate to. They have character defects just like everybody does. But it's how they strive to overcome them and do the right thing, is what I hope to convey in their stories going forward in the Death in Hawaii Series.

During the twenty-two years I lived on the big island, I witnessed some amazing things. Those events are where a lot of the inspiration I get comes from. My goal is to intersperse those moments in my books creating something unique that you can only get when you read my stories.

Hawaii is a magical place, my words will never do it justice. I hope that readers of the Death in Hawaii series take away a bit of aloha after spending time with Sam and Jessica.

Get the free prequel and new release notifications.

https://readerlinks.com/l/965413

HAWAIIAN GLOSSARY

Mana (Ma-Na)
Spirit
Aina (Eye-Na)
Land of the island.
Beach Boys
They light the resort's tiki torches, pull the pig from the imu and help tourists safely enjoy the beach.
Honu (Ho-Nu)
It is a green sea turtle.
Malama (Ma-La-ma)
To take care of.
Hapa (Ha-Pa)
Means mixed race. Hawaiian, Chinese, Japanese, Portuguese and Filipino make up the majority of the population in Hawaii and when they marry their children are called hapa. A mixture.

Huli-huli chicken is grilled on a trailer in a parking lot or on the side of the road. It's usually related to a fundraiser.

Da-Kine (dah-KINE) is a fill in word used for anything you can't remember the name of.

Aloha (ah-LOH-hah)

Aloha is "hello" and "goodbye." You could also have the spirit of aloha = Giving, caring.

Mahalo (mah-HA-loh)

Means "thank you."

Haole (HOW-leh)

It's used to refer to white people. It can be used offensively, but isn't always meant to be insulting. Originally it meant foreigner, but I seriously doubt anyone uses it for that anymore.

Kane (KAH-neh)

Kane refers to men or boys.

Wahine (wah-HEE-neh)

Wahine refers to women or girls.

Keiki (KAY-kee)

This word means "child." You may hear locals call their children "keiki."

Hale (HAH-leh)

Hale translates to "home" or "house." It can often refer to housing in general.

Pau (POW)

When you put the soy sauce bottle down, you may hear a local ask, "Are you pau with that?" Pau essentially means "finished" or "done."

Howzit (HOW-zit)

In Hawaii, "howzit" is a common pidgin greeting that translates to "hello" or "how are you?"

Lolo (loh-loh)

When someone calls you "lolo," they're saying you're "crazy or dumb." It's sometimes used in a teasing manner.

Ono (OH-noh)

Ono means "delicious." It can often be paired with the pidgin word "grinds," which translates to "food." So, if you eat something delicious, you might say it's ono grinds.

Ohana (oh-HAH-nah)

Means family.

Tita (tit-uh)

Refers to a woman or teenage girl who could be said to either be a tomboy or else somewhat aggressive, tough, or rough with her language or manners.

Tutu (too-too)

Means grand mother. Google says it references both grand parents, but I've never heard that on the island.

BOATING GLOSSARY

Saloon = Living room. The social area of a larger boat is called the *saloon*. However, it is pronounced "salon."

Cockpit = Is a name for the location of controls of a vessel; while traditionally an open well in the deck of a boat outside any deckhouse or cabin, in modern boats they may refer to an enclosed area.

Head = Is the bathroom.

Galley = Kitchen.

Stateroom = Bedroom.

Bulkhead = Wall.

Line = Rope.

Port = Standing at the rear of a boat and looking forward, "port" refers to the entire left side of the boat.

Starboard = Standing at the rear of a boat and looking forward, "starboard" refers to the entire right side of the boat.

B.O.A.T. = Bust Out Another Thousand$

COPYRIGHT

Made in the USA
Coppell, TX
05 August 2022

80968636R00111